take me in bali

KD ELIZABETH

TAKE ME ABROAD BOOK ONE

VLM

ISBN:
ISBN-13: 978-1-956045-04-8 (paperback)

Editing: Cassie Pearse
Proofreading: Red Leaf Proofing
Cover Design: K.D. Elizabeth
Print and E-book Formatting: K.D. Elizabeth

For they
who choose a different life.

CHAPTER ONE

SCHILLER

The man is already staring at me the moment I sit down. Even in the crowded bar, one of the few air-conditioned places in this town, his direct gaze sticks out. I'm used to the attention, unfortunately, but this man does it with such particular impunity it really grates.

I ignore him.

The waitress finally brings our drinks, weaving around the well-dressed bodies that have somehow managed not to melt in the over eighty-degree heat, so much worse for all the humidity. She smiles at me suggestively—which I also ignore—and then flounces away when I don't instantly succumb to her charms. Before she has a chance to leave, however, I sling back my Scotch and return the glass, wordlessly asking for another.

"That was an eighty-dollar glass of Scotch, bro," says my friend, Bentley.

I shrug. "It's been a helluva week."

Helluva month, rather. No, decade. Ever since I gave my family the final fuck-off ten years ago, it's been one shit-storm after the next. Defying one of America's titans of industry outright is never a great idea—even more so when you're the heir apparent. Still, the stuffy waters of Rhode Island are a far cry from these blissful beaches of Bali. Sometimes it's hard to remember that Newport even exists on the same planet as this place.

Bentley sips his own drink much more sedately than I did—an actual accomplishment coming from him—and says, "Well, at least the job is over."

I groan. "Couldn't have come soon enough. If I have to teach just *one* more spoiled third wife how to dive, I'm going to—"

"Give it all up," Bentley finishes, rolling his eyes. "No, you will not. They'd have to lock you up entirely to keep you out of the water. Even if that means certifying idiots, apparently. Don't get it, myself. Why deal with the wives when it's not as if you need to work a day in your life? That's just straight-up masochism, dude."

"Hardly. And unlike you, I don't have any desire to while away my life, my brain slowly rotting from too much booze, women, and other less palatable activities."

Bentley grins the boyish smirk that has gotten many said women into trouble. "But it's so fun, though."

I smile thinly and say nothing. Over the many years of our friendship, Bentley and I have diverged in how we view our respective fortunes. While I resent my wealth, Bentley flaunts his shamelessly. Sometimes it's a point of contention between us, but these days we've agreed to disagree. It's the only way to remain friends.

And I desperately need a friend right now.

"Well," says Bentley quietly once the waitress has returned with my second drink, "we won't go there again. You have some time off now, right? Tell me we can get a halfway decent place this time."

I roll my eyes. Bentley's idea of something halfway decent would bankrupt most people. "Yes, fine. We won't slum it. After the week I've just had, I couldn't cope with anything less. The wife came onto me not once, not twice, but *four* separate times—"

"Wow, such a hardship, Schiller. A real shame."

"In front of her husband. Who was virtually senile."

Bentley winces.

"Yeah," I say. "She was not subtle. At all."

Bentley grins. "Maybe they've got a thing going with single, attractive young males."

"Christ, don't put that picture in my mind. The image might ruin this drink, and it's a damn good one."

"Schiller?"

Our heads jerk up. A man makes his way toward us, sticking out from the crowd not only because his comfortable clothing is worn, but also because he's clearly a local.

"Hey, man," I grin, pulling out the chair next to me. "You made it."

Bentley glances at me. "You know this guy?"

"Made," I say, "Pronounced like 'ma' and 'day' together but spelled like 'made.' He worked on the crew last week

3

and when I realized he can actually dive, I decided to hire him away from that nightmare of a yacht to show me around some decent dive sites on my time off."

"You mean during the week I'm going to be here?" Bentley says. "Dude, you do know I flew to the opposite end of the earth for you, don't you?"

I clap him on the shoulder. "So come with. You're certified. We'll come back to shore each night so you can get your fill of the nightlife."

Bentley tips his glass under my nose. "You can't drink if you're going to dive the next day, you ass."

"Like that's ever stopped you."

"True," Bentley muses, staring into the glass.

"I can sit?"

I turn my attention to Made. "Of course. What do you want to drink?"

He shakes his head. "I'm leading a dive tomorrow morning. But thanks."

Made looks around the nightclub as Bentley throws a capitulating glance my way and groans before throwing back his drink and saying, "Looks like I better enjoy tonight, then."

"I've never been inside here before," says Made. "It's ... loud."

I snort. "That it is. Bentley insisted."

"Hey, I didn't *insist*—"

"Your very existence here and the fact that I know you, were essentially an insistence."

"Fuck you, man," Bentley says without heat, flipping

me off and then catching the attention of the waitress for another round.

Made's gaze flicks over my shoulder. "Uh, Schiller, do you know—"

"There's a man staring at me?" I say, taking another sip. "Yeah, I'm well aware."

"Do you ... know him?" Made says, something peculiar flashing in his eyes.

"No," I say dryly, "but I'm hoping if I ignore him long enough, he'll get the picture. I'm sure he'll make his way over here before long, anyway."

Bentley takes his new drink from the waitress and stares over my shoulder. "Who's this, now?"

"Don't look!" I hiss. "It'll only encourage him."

"Aw, shit, man," Bentley says, wincing again. "Too late."

"Great," I mumble into my drink. Hopefully whatever this is won't take long, but if it's about what I suspect it is, that's doubtful.

"You are Schiller Tate, yes?"

I place my glass carefully on the table, not bothering to look up at the man now standing right behind me. "That is correct."

"I would very much like to speak with you."

"Sorry, not interested," I say. The man, however, completely ignores me and stalks around the table before neatly folding himself into the chair directly opposite me.

He's clad in a blindingly white linen suit, somehow entirely free of wrinkles. A matching white fedora with a blue stripe around the rim is perched on his head, brown hair curling at his nape and contrasting remarkably with the utter paleness of his skin. He pulls a cigar from his breast pocket and lights it, turning his head to blow the smoke almost directly into Made's face, his eyes never leaving mine.

Pompous shit. Fuck whatever it is this guy wants.

"I am not interested in whatever you have to offer me," I say coldly.

He shrugs indolently, puffing on the cigar. He extends his hand toward me, which I decline to shake. He shrugs again. "I assure you; I'll make it worth your while."

"And I assure you that I'm not interested. Now, if you'll excuse us, we'd like to get back to our evening."

"You *are* the Schiller Tate of Tate Shipping, are you not?" says the man with the blasé tone of a person who already knows the answer. "I thought I recognized you."

"I cannot put you in contact with my father, and I have no desire to make investments of my own," I say flatly.

Something like a smile tilts the corners of his mouth. "Oh, it's not your father I'm interested in, boy."

"How surprising, considering you're around the same age as him."

The smile is more than a hint now, and all the more irritating for it. "Yes, I suppose youth has rather passed me by, hasn't it? You'd do well to remember that, Tate. You'd be, what, thirty-four by now?"

"Read my Wikipedia page, did you?"

"Of a sort."

"Look, man, I can see that you've got something to say,"

Bentley says, "but my friend's just not interested, okay? Move on out, now."

The man blows another mouthful of smoke at Made, who remains absolutely still. "The name's Miles Lachlan. I represent a group of people who are interested in going after the *Galvanizer*."

Bentley winces, Made glances from Lachlan to my friend, but I don't give him the satisfaction of a reaction.

Lachlan turns his attention to Bentley. "You must know the story."

Bentley says nothing.

Lachlan swings his gaze to Made. "But you probably don't. A local, are you? How curious. Are you helping Tate with his own expedition, then? There could be no other reason for his being here."

"Why don't you just come out with it," I snap.

Lachlan smiles a nasty grin. "Fine. I am heading a three-week expedition to find the wreck. I heard you're the guy to lead it. So, here I am. I won't take no for an answer. Particularly not with your *special* background."

My jaw clenches. "If you've heard that, then you must have also heard that I've failed. Multiple times. Without the slightest success. Why attempt such a futile endeavor?"

Lachlan chuckles. "When a yacht goes down with one hundred million dollars in precious metals and fine art aboard, the reason should be self-apparent."

"It went down in 1992."

Lachlan nods. "Precisely. The value of the wreck would

be well north of a hundred million by now, nearly thirty years later."

"One might argue that if it hasn't been found yet, it likely won't be. The art alone is surely ruined."

"Perhaps."

"And you want me to find it," I say.

"Correct."

"No."

Lachlan blinks, like he's never been outright refused before. "I would make it very well worth your time."

I lean forward, placing my forearms on the table and glaring at him. "That wreck is a damn ghost. No one knew Galvan's final destination. It's only rumored that he docked in this general area the week before his ship went down. No one knows for sure.

"In three decades, despite probably hundreds of people looking for this ship, no one has even been able to find wreckage, let alone the entire wreck, let alone the so-called treasure. This time, with you, would be no different. You are wasting your time. I'm not interested."

"Oh, it would be different this time."

I consider him. Everyone always says that when they first hire me; inevitably, they're disappointed. Something about this asshole's demeanor has me thinking there might be more lurking here, though.

Something's off.

"Be that as it may," I say slowly, "I must refuse. I've wasted far too much of my life on that wreck. I'm done with it now. You'll have to find someone else."

Lachlan takes another puff on the cigar, his gaze locked with mine. After a long moment, he says, "I will pay you five thousand American dollars per day, plus all living expenses aboard, of course. And the best dive equipment money can buy will be at your disposal."

"I have my own gear."

He shrugs. "Of course. But I was referring to the rest. Lift bags. Metal detectors. LiDAR satellite technology in addition to the standard SONAR. Et cetera. I presume you don't keep those in your checked luggage, no?"

Even Bentley gives a low whistle. Made looks like he's about to faint. They're right to be surprised; LiDAR is some sophisticated shit. Some sophisticated, *expensive* shit. The technology sends pulsed lasers into the water to give a three-dimensional reading of the ocean floor. Hundreds of wrecks have been found all around the world.

It's even been used to find previously undiscovered Maya ruins in Central America, where no human being has trod for decades, if not centuries. The technology proved valuable enough that companies put so much research into it that the technology evolved. Now you can find it in all tablets sold by a company that has the same name as a fruit, for example.

Point being, LiDAR is not amateur hour. So either this guy's yanking my chain—or he knows something I don't.

My eyes narrow.

Lachlan smiles smugly. "And upon finding the wreck, I will pay you another hundred thousand as a bonus."

Now I *know* he's up to something. No one throws that

kind of money around for an adventure dive. This guy means business.

Lachlan climbs to his feet, putting out his cigar in Bentley's now-empty glass. "Think about it. We'll be departing from Sanur two days from now. Your friends here are welcome to join the trip as my guests as well. Be sure to find us at the port the morning of our departure should you like to help pick the crew and dive team."

He disappears into the crowd.

Bentley stares after him. "That guy's a dick."

"You don't say."

"Schiller," Made says quietly. "You cannot work for that man."

"Why not?" I ask.

"He's not from around here, but once he came over from Australia, it wasn't long before he took over the island. It's rumored—he's involved, yes? Involved with very bad people. He's put locals out of jobs and bought out the homes of others to put up huge hotels, restaurants. Everything.

"If he can't bribe an official to get the permit, he threatens them. I'm sure what he's unofficially done is even worse. Whatever he wants, don't give it to him. Stay well away. Only the most desperate locals will be tempted by that absurd sum. Inevitably, he'll find a crew, but you don't want to be one of those people."

"Well, great," says Bentley. "Exactly what I wanted to do on my much-needed Balinese vacation. Christ, I need another drink. Let's forget all this, Schill. Okay? What we need is a nice spa, yeah? Some beautiful yoga instructors. A rice terrace or two. Volcanoes. Forget the beaches; let's explore the inner island. Dive next week. You're not going to shrivel up without daily saltwater. Ubud should be bangin', right?"

I remain silent.

Bentley groans. "No. Schiller? No. Look, I get it, man. He's after that damn wreck and you failed to dissuade him. But you agree to work for this crime lord, and then I'll have to feel all obligated to go along just to make sure you're fine. If I get kidnapped, my father will *kill me* if he has to pay a ransom. Again. Last time that happened he liquidated it out of my trust and purposely sold the cheapest shares. I got absolutely annihilated on the capital gains tax. Think of my children's inheritance, Schill. Be a good friend."

"If you ever have children," I say, "I will personally call Child Protective Services myself."

Bentley rolls his eyes. "Dude, you know I'm right. This shit is no business of ours."

I drum my fingers on the table.

Bentley sighs. "You're totally going to do this, aren't you?"

"Yep."

He shakes his head and pantomimes throttling me. "Damn you. I was supposed to be here for a nice week of relaxing with my bro before heading on to Singapore. And now this shit. You know this means I now have to cancel my plans and stay here with you, don't you? If I don't, you're going to go off all half-cocked and then three weeks from now, I'll read in some international headline that you ended up at the bottom of the sea or some shit. I can't have that on my conscience. You better get me an *extra* special Christmas gift this year."

I grin, glad he'll be staying with me. Because as well as I know him, Bentley knows me just as well. And while I might pretend I want nothing to do with that wreck, he knows that's a lie. And he definitely knows I'll need the moral support.

Because the real reason everyone always wants to hire me to find the sunken remains of the *Galvanizer* is the same reason I want *no one* to find it.

Lawrence Galvan was my godfather.

CHAPTER TWO

PIPPA

"Get out of my hostel at once!"

I jerk awake so hard I fall out of bed; fortunately for me, I was assigned the lower bunk, or the fall might have hurt me. Rolling over in a daze, I blink up at the hostel owner standing over me, still half-asleep.

"Wha—"

"Get OUT!" He jabs a finger down at me, so furious he's literally spitting mad.

I clutch my thin blanket over me; it's absurdly hot in Bali, so I only sleep in really short shorts and a thin camisole. That, plus the rude awakening is enough to set me off.

"Excuse me, but perhaps you might want to speak to me like an actual human being and allow me to first put on proper clothing before you yell at me. Being in the women's dorm this early in the morning is absolutely unacceptable.

You wouldn't want someone to lodge a formal complaint, would you?"

Indeed, the other women in the room are peering at him uncomfortably while they hide under their blankets.

The owner pauses, glances around. His face slowly turns purple as he realizes I have a damn good point. He jabs a finger at me again. "Get your shit together and meet me downstairs in five minutes. And if you don't, the only formal complaint that will be lodged will be me against *you*."

He storms from the room.

"What did you do?" a girl asks from the top bunk in the corner, eyes wide, as I pull on yesterday's clothes and begin packing up all of my belongings.

"No idea," I mumble, shoving the rest of my items in my backpack and zipping it closed. Finished, I straighten and address the bunk above me. "Hey, Mel—"

She's not there.

I stare at the empty bed. Mel is no early riser. In fact, she's almost always the last person into bed every night. At —I glance at my battered dive watch—*six-thirty* in the morning, no way should she be anywhere else but sleeping in that bed.

Oh shit.

The girls send me sympathetic glances as I trudge from the room. I *knew* I should have trusted my first impression of her. It's not often, though, that I find a female backpacker my age. For the last few chows, we've been traveling together through Indonesia after running into each other in

Jakarta. After multiple mortifying incidents of her being rude, inconsiderate, or just outright manipulative, I've wondered if it might be time to cut the cord.

Looks like the time is now.

The owner is seething right outside the door when I exit the room, arms crossed over his chest. He grabs my arm roughly and starts hauling me toward the stairs.

"Do *not* touch me," I snarl, ripping my arm away. He huffs in annoyance and grumbles as I follow him down into his office.

"Now, what's—"

"Your friend stole two thousand dollars from me! All of the money I had locked in my safe, gone. All of it. Your partner did it."

I gape at him. "How do you—"

"There's a camera in this office pointed directly at the safe! See?" He points behind my head.

My eyes scan the top of the filing cabinet. All I see is a figurine of the Uluwatu temple and a potted plant. "I don't understand what I'm supposed to be looking at."

"There's a camera hidden inside the figurine! I had to put it up there after the last time I was robbed. I've watched her breaking in three times already this morning. She's clearly a professional; that's no cheap safe. I'm sure the only reason she didn't disable the camera is because it's hidden so well. And you were with her. You must pay me the two thousand, or I'm calling the police."

I rear back. "That's ridiculous. I had nothing to do with it."

"You were with her. You're her accomplice."

"I'm nothing of the sort! I only met the woman three weeks ago. Look, it's awful that she did this, but be reasonable. Why would I help her steal from you and then climb back into bed like nothing happened? If I'd been involved, I would have left as well.

"While I certainly hope that you catch her, I think it would be best if I checked out early. I don't appreciate your insinuation that I'm guilty by association, and I *especially* don't like your treatment of me this morning. You better believe that will be reflected in my review. Women traveling alone should be aware that you find it acceptable to barge into their rooms early in the morning while they're still sleeping. I believe I owe you for the last three days?"

The owner hems and haws while I sling my pack off my shoulder and search inside for my wallet, going on about how his establishment is perfectly safe for all people, including women, and that he never would have been in the room in the first place if this hadn't happened.

Whatever. You don't travel for over a decade like I have and keep putting up with such boorishness. I have come across many an asshole hostel owner; I've long ago stopped caring at all whether I piss someone off. Someone's got to stand up for the eighteen-and nineteen-year-old girls traveling around on a gap year like the ones I just left in that room upstairs.

Pulling my wallet out, I open it to give him what I owe for the last couple nights. What the—my wallet is empty! I search all of its pockets even though I never keep my bills anywhere but in the main one. Nothing.

I'm completely cleaned out. All of the remaining money I had from my last job crewing a yacht from Kuala Lumpur to Jakarta is gone. Apart from the sixty dollars in local currency I religiously keep hidden in my underwear for emergencies, I don't have a penny to my name.

That *bitch*. She didn't just clear out this asshole; she stole from me as well.

At least she left my passport. I would have really been fucked in that case. But what if she—I sprint to the row of lockers shoved up along the opposite wall and dial the combination on my padlock. Ripping the door open, I paw through all my equipment, practically wilting against the locker when I confirm that all of my dive gear is present.

Thank God she didn't think to steal any of my gear. Mel's not a diver, so she must not have thought of the possibility of reselling my gear, which easily costs three times what she stole from this guy. This dive equipment is the only thing of value I possess. If she'd somehow managed to break off my lock and taken that too, I would have been beyond inconsolable.

It's taken me years to piece it together, scrimped from meager savings I accumulated from one crappy job after another. It's all I have to show for the nearly thirteen years of working various odd jobs around the world.

I've gone without meals to save for various pieces of this equipment. I've seen some of the most unbelievably beautiful places on this planet using this stuff. I don't even know who I'd be without it. If she'd taken even one piece, I would have hunted Mel to the ends of the earth to get it back on principle alone.

Which arrives at my next problem. I bet this guy knows *exactly* how valuable this gear is, since he books dive charters for people staying here every day.

I slowly turn back to him. He's still raging about the injustice of the situation, which is understandable, but I just don't deserve the brunt of all that anger.

"How much did I owe you?" I say quietly, resigned. He glares at me, then quotes a figure equivalent to about fifty dollars. I wince. That's virtually everything I have on me.

"Look," I say slowly, showing him my wallet. "She robbed me, too. See? Everything I had left from my last job is gone."

He barely glances at my wallet. "How is that my problem? Your friend robs me of two thousand dollars, and you expect me to let you skip out of here without paying as well? No."

"She's not my friend."

His eyes narrow. "Are you saying you don't have it?"

Technically I do but paying him would just about clear me out. Until I can get another job, paying him would leave me with about ten dollars to my name. Not exactly fun.

Of course, there's another way I could pay my way out of this situation, but I refuse to take that route.

"Could you give me a week to get it to you?"

He scoffs.

"Two days?"

He rolls his eyes. "If you're in such a bad situation, I suppose I could take some of that dive gear off your hands. I could probably get a few bucks for it."

That asshole. He'd get a hell of a lot more than that, and we both know it.

"Not happening."

He smiles grimly. "Well, if you don't have it, then we seem to have a bit of a problem. I suppose I'll need to call the police, after all."

"That won't be necessary," I say through gritted teeth. Digging into my pack, I remove my emergency fund from my underwear and hand over the necessary amount, wincing as I do. I am going to kill Mel if I ever come across her again. It's been a long time since I've been so duped.

The owner makes a big show of counting it out; I barely prevent myself from rolling my eyes. What a terrible human being; I get he's upset about being robbed, and I can't say that I blame him, but he doesn't need to take it out on me.

"Get your shit," he growls.

I barely have time to grab my backpack and gear before he throws me out of his hostel. It's still early enough that all the tourists are sleeping; only locals are up right now. They stare at me as I'm shoved off the premises, and the man screams at me that if he ever sees my face again, he'll call the police.

Now what?

A job. I need a job immediately. I groan; this grind isn't as fun as it used to be. I've lived hand-to-mouth since I was eighteen, barely eking out a living on the various jobs I've worked. I started out working for room and board, but as I gained experience over the years, I began to earn some wages, which allowed me to cobble together the dive gear. That finally gave me the ability to start getting much better jobs, which paid, if not amazing wages, certainly enough to let me continue traveling around the world without the sword of starvation perpetually hanging over my head.

My last job even paid so well that I decided to take an entire month off—how I ended up traveling around Indonesia in the first place. My plan had been to spend my last week diving around the island before finding some other job, but apparently there will be no diving for me in Bali.

"Excuse me, miss?"

I turn. A local stands before me, an older gentleman with a sympathetic look on his face. "Yes?"

"I couldn't help but overhear. You got kicked out?"

"Worse than that," I mutter. "I got robbed, too."

His sympathetic expression deepens. "I'm sorry that happened. We always hope people will have a nice time here in Bali."

"Oh, it's not like that," I rush to reply. "It was the woman who was traveling with me who stole all my money. I met her a few weeks ago, and apparently was a terrible judge of character. I don't suppose you would happen to know where I could find some immediate work, would you?"

He gives me a considering look. "Do you have any skills?"

"I've crewed boats for the last ten years now," I say. "And I'm a certified diver."

He brightens. "Oh! Then go to Sanur. Many of the foreign yachts come into port there. Almost always someone is looking for work. You might be able to find something for a few days."

"Great," I say, trying to sound enthused. Sanur is all the way across the island, and I have no way to get there. No inexpensive way with all this gear, that is. "Thanks for the tip."

"I could drive you, if you like?"

My eyes narrow. Why is this guy so helpful? "That's too generous."

The man pats my arm. "It's okay; I'm going there myself. My son is heading out on a trip, and I'm going to see him off. He is also a diver. Perhaps he could find you something. See, this is his photo."

He shows me a picture of a seemingly harmless man roughly around my age. He looks legit. If this is all an elaborate con, then it's quite a detailed one. While the smarter thing to do would be to find some other way to get to the port at Sanur, I doubt anyone else would offer a free ride. I'll have to risk it.

Reluctantly agreeing, the man, who introduces himself as Wayan, helps me load my dive gear and pack into his tiny car as I climb into the seat beside him. Wayan tells stories of his wife and four children as we barrel through the busy roads, the infernally hot breeze blasting me full in the face through the open window of a car that has no air conditioning.

BY THE TIME we arrive in Sanur, I'm already exhausted. Wayan says I can keep my belongings in his car while I look for work, since his son is still making preparations to get underway and doesn't have time yet to say goodbye to his father. I remove my passport and wallet from my pack, then begin making my way up and down each row of the port, asking anyone if they have work available.

It soon becomes apparent that no one is hiring, which isn't surprising. It's the middle of the week, so most people who've chartered for at least seven days are already out to sea by now, and all the day trips will be coming in soon for the day.

I canvass the port with increasing desperation. If I can't find something soon, I'll be forced to do something I swore I'd never do: Take money from someone who will forever hold it over me.

I've very nearly resigned myself to giving up when shouts erupt from the other end of the docks. A large crowd is gathered at a slip where a hundred-thirty-foot mega yacht is docked.

It's a beautiful ship; the kind of vessel I've lived aboard on many an occasion and yet will never hope of owning myself. I size it up in a glance. Three levels, likely at least four decently-sized cabins, a surely ostentatious stateroom for whoever owns the yacht, quarters for the crew, a spacious galley, impressive aft deck and huge bay for holding all kinds of water toys.

In other words, a dreamboat of a yacht for divers like me.

I practically sprint over. Most of the assembled people are locals, all yelling over one another to draw the attention of the immaculately dressed man standing on the dock above them. His linen suit is spotless; his fedora tipped so low the brim hides one side of his face. He gazes down at the crowd below him, a satisfied smile curving his mouth as if enjoying being the cause of all this ruckus.

"What's this about?" I ask a man standing next to me.

He jerks his chin toward the man. "That guy's hirin' a whole crew for that whale of a ship of his. Goin' treasure hunting."

I laugh. "No, really. Why is he hiring?"

He stares at me.

I gape. "You are not serious."

"Why would I lie, lady?" He nods toward the man again. "That guy's goin' treasure huntin' for two or three weeks, and he's willing to hire a crew at five hundred U.S. dollars a day to do it. People are practically killing each other to get a slot."

"No way," I bark. Five hundred a *day*? That's an absurd amount to pay any crew member. If the charter lasts three weeks, I'd have nearly ten grand to play with. I could travel around this part of the world for *months* on that amount of money—and live like a king.

I must get on that yacht.

"What are they hiring?" I ask casually.

The man laughs. "I highly doubt they'd need a pretty girl like yourself."

Well, fuck him, then. I push through the crowd, worming my way closer in time to hear the man proclaim that they've already hired the last crew member. A wave of protests erupts from the crowd. I slump in disappointment; if I'd only started on this end of the port, I might have gotten a spot.

"Sorry, folks!" the man calls. "We've got everyone we need. Most of the positions got filled early this morning. We're just waiting on our steward to arrive, and then we'll be underway."

The man turns and makes to walk down the dock toward his vessel. My eyes follow him, and I nearly turn away myself when my gaze snags on the back of the boat. One of the newly hired crew is loading crate after crate of dive gear into the stern. Tanks, weights, lift bags. The whole deal. That man was right; these guys really *are* looking for something.

"Wait!" I cry, leaping up onto the dock behind him. He turns, smiling slightly in amusement.

"Yes?"

"You need a steward," I say.

His amusement deepens. "No, I said we were waiting on her. We don't need one."

"But she's not here," I say. Ordinarily, I'd feel bad about blatantly attempting to steal some other woman's job, but my circumstances are just too dire. This guy's a foreigner; he speaks English, he's got cash to blow. The job has practically dropped down out of the sky, and I do not intend to let the opportunity pass.

He gives me a speculative look. "That is true. She's not here."

I glance at the gear again. "Seems to me like she's late."

The man turns to face me fully now, hands tucked insouciantly inside his pockets. "I suppose that's true as well. But she had until they finished loading to show up, so technically she's not late. Yet."

I jerk my head toward the boat. "I'm also a steward."

"Are you now?"

"Yes," I say, trying to keep the desperation out of my tone. "I've crewed vessels in Monaco, Mykonos, and the Seychelles, to name a few, for over a decade. Just did Kuala Lumpur to Jakarta. I could not be more qualified. I assure you, whoever you have already isn't as good as I am. She's not even *here*."

The man's head cocks, that irritating smile still painting his lips. "You're a pretty little thing, aren't you? I do like your gumption."

I grind my teeth in the effort not to lay into him; not only are his sexist words offensive, but I'm nearly six feet tall—not exactly a "little thing" by any stretch of the imagination. But I remain silent; I can stroke an ego to suit my purposes like the best of them.

The man shrugs. "Regrettably, we just don't have room for you."

He turns toward his ship.

"Wait!" I cry again. He slowly turns, still smiling, as if he knows exactly how badly I need this job, and that reality entertains him. "I'm a certified diver. You're going after something, right? You need a whole dive crew. I have my own gear and am a certified master diver. *And* I'm a steward. Wouldn't you prefer to have someone aboard who can do two jobs? Look," I add, pointing toward Wayan's vehicle. "My gear is all there, just waiting to go. I could be on board and ready to get underway within five minutes. Isn't the tide going out? You're going to want to give way soon."

He smiles wide. "All right, then. Bring your stuff aboard. We're going after the *Galvanizer*."

CHAPTER THREE

PIPPA

I return to Wayan after the owner disappears onto his yacht, leaving me gaping on the dock. While I've managed to talk my way into some cushy jobs over the years, this one is easily up there in the top five. In a few short weeks, I'll net ten grand and be able to travel wherever I want for the foreseeable future.

And I'll even be able to get some diving in while aboard! Excellent.

"Were you able to find work?" Wayan asks when I rejoin him.

"Actually, I did," I say. "See that vessel down at the other end? I'm going to be a steward aboard for a few weeks."

Wayan's gaze follows where I'm pointing. "That ship there?"

I nod.

A troubled look steals over his face. "That is the boat of Miles Lachlan."

"He owns it?"

"Yes."

"I guess that's who I just spoke to, then."

Wayan glances at me. "You spoke to him? Alone?"

Trepidation flashes through me. "Is there a problem?"

Wayan considers. "This job ... how badly do you need it?"

The trepidation grows. "About as badly as one could need a job."

"As I thought." Wayan frowns, and stares at me. "You must promise me, Miss Pippa, to never be alone with that man."

"*What?*"

"That man is ... a criminal. He is a bad man."

"Well, *great*," I groan. "That's probably why that other steward never showed up."

"Possibly."

"Do you think I should decline the job?" I ask.

Wayan shrugs. "It would be better if you did, but you need the money, yes? That's why we work for him, too. My son? He will be working on the boat as well. A big diver like you. Very good. You tell him I said to watch out for you. I will do so as well when I say goodbye to him. Always stick close to him, and you should be fine. They will have a couple of foreigners on the boat, so I am sure you will be left alone. But stay close to Made."

I turn to stare at the yacht. Do I risk it? Do I really

have any other choice? Sure, the man had seemed like an asshole, but a criminal? I hadn't gotten *that* particular vibe.

Wayan motions for my phone, which I grip tightly with sudden anxiety. "Give me your phone. This is my number. If there is service aboard and something goes wrong, you call me, yes? I will send someone for you. Remember, I want my son to be okay as well."

I nod. This is likely as good as it's going to get. And if we're looking for the *Galvanizer*, chances are there will be other boats in the area trying to find it as well. Worse comes to worst, I can take refuge on one of them.

Squeezing Wayan's shoulder, I say, "Thank you, Wayan. I can't—you've done more for me than you know."

"Watch out for my son, yes? He can take care of himself, but a father worries."

"Of course."

Wayan helps me pile my gear at the end of the dock.

"Made!" he calls.

The man I saw piling gear onto the boat looks up. He waves in greeting and walks along the deck to us. Made. He's a little older than in the photo Wayan had, but I still recognize him.

"Father. I told you not to come," he calls down from the boat.

Wayan smiles. "Yes, well, I had to. You are determined to go, then?"

Made frowns. "Yes, Father. It is my job."

Wayan's expression turns unhappy. "As I expected. In

that case, please watch over Miss Pippa during the trip. This is my son, Made."

"Pleasure to meet you," I say.

Made glances from me to his father. "Pardon me, but are you coming aboard?"

"Yes," I huff, lugging my tank over. "Could you help me load this? With the rest I should be fine."

"I'm not sure I follow," he says.

"Lachlan replaced the steward with me."

"Oh. In that case, allow me." He leans over, extending his hands. I pass him my tank, which he puts at his feet, then hand him my pony bottle, a smaller tank that attaches near my hip and acts as a reserve in case my main tank runs out of air. He looks from the pony and then to me, respect flashing across his face, which I silently acknowledge.

Most divers never pass the recreational diver stage; they dive their whole lives on one tank. Technical divers, however, usually dive on more than one tank so in the event that something happens to their system or they become separated from their dive partner they have an alternate source of air. Divers refer to this system as a bailout.

I'm somewhere in the middle; having gone up and a little beyond the recreational diver levels, my system is more complex than the average diver's. But I'm nowhere near the *truly* advanced stuff, where people dive caves or wrecks hundreds of feet below the surface and might take hours to come up safely after taking just five minutes to descend.

Interesting that this man picked up on it. Most of the divers I meet on boats are certainly experienced with the recreational stuff, but anything more is generally outside their wheelhouse.

"You know, Made, your name seems unusual," I say once I've handed all my gear over to him. "I've never heard of it outside Bali."

They roar with laughter.

"Um ... I wasn't trying to joke?"

Made waves a hand, then places my tanks with the others already stowed. "It's just ... you couldn't know how funny that was."

"Perhaps you could explain it to me?"

Still chuckling, Wayan says, "In Bali we name our children after their birth order. The oldest child is named either Wayan, Putu, or Gede. The second oldest—that's me—is Made, Kadek, or Nengah. Then comes Nyoman and Komang for the third child. And then Ketut for the fourth. And if you have a fifth child, it would be Wayan Balik, which translated for you would mean something like 'Wayan Again.'"

I grin, getting it now. "So when I said that was an unusual name—"

"It is in fact the second most common on this island, yes," Made finishes, smiling.

"I will leave you to your work. Please do be careful, son. And remember, you have my number, Miss Pippa," says Wayan. With a wave, he heads back to his car.

Made and I watch him go. I turn to him. "You know, he also told me to watch out for you, too."

Made chuckles. "Of course he did. Well, you won't

need to worry about me. As for you ... I'll keep Lachlan away."

"Should be rather difficult when I'll be serving him his meals," I joke. "At least I'll be able to get some diving in after all."

Made's head jerks toward me. "Oh, you won't be diving."

I stare at him. "But he hired me over the girl who never showed specifically because I mentioned I dive."

"Yes, but Lachlan is a sexist. Among other things. He's already hired the dive team. He doesn't need another diver. Believe me, I was there when Tate selected them this morning. Lachlan hired you because you're pretty, and he likes pretty things. I'll make sure your gear's stowed properly, but I'd be shocked if you use it once these next few weeks."

"Are you serious?" I say, furious.

"Yes, very."

"And who's Tate?"

"Schiller Tate. The divemaster for this expedition. He's the one planning out all the dives, who looks for what. Where we go down. He's got more experience searching for the *Galvanizer* than anyone else on this planet; it's his show, and you and I are merely along for the ride. Well, it's really Lachlan's show, but he's actually deferring to Tate in this area. For now, anyway.

"Tate carefully selected his entire team. He was really particular about who he picked; insisted on seeing them all dive prior to hiring them on. You, unfortunately, have not been tested, so no way Tate lets you get in the water.

Lachlan knows that, too. So when I say he only hired you for your face—"

"That's really why he hired me," I finish. "Bastard."

Made shrugs. "That he is, unfortunately. Just do your job and avoid him, yes? He won't—can't do anything to you, not with all these people aboard. There's Tate, for one. He'd never allow that. And Tate brought a friend, who seems ... self-absorbed, but likely wouldn't allow it either."

"Not to mention *I* would not allow it," I say through gritted teeth.

Made shrugs again. "Yes, yes. But it never hurts to have allies. For me, as well. Locals can get the short end of the stick if something goes wrong in situations like these."

I frown. "That's not right, either."

"It is the way of life. But in three weeks, we will both have a stack of cash, yes? So let's keep our heads down, and then after, I'll take you to all the great dive locations off Bali and Lombok. The *real* spots—not just the tourist traps."

I smile, then hold out a hand. "That sounds like a plan."

Made shakes my hand and smiles as well, then nods toward the cabin. "You should head inside, get settled. The chef will probably want to meet you soon. Crew's quarters are last door on the left. I'll be busy getting us underway, but maybe I'll see you later."

"Thanks, Made."

Heading for the cabin, I duck inside and make for the quarters. The inside of the vessel is as gorgeous as its outside, full of beautiful wood paneling cut in clean lines without any ostentatious detailing. That's actually a bit strange. I would have thought Lachlan would be the kind of person—

I slam into someone.

"What the—"

"Oh, sorry I—"

My apology dies a quick death the instant I lift my face to the person I've just walked into. Full lips, a straight and austere nose, square jaw that looks like it could cut granite, and tousled black hair stare down at me. The most incredible thing is that they *are* staring down at me. I'm only a couple inches shy of six feet, and this guy must have me by at least five inches. I'm so unused to looking up at someone it's honestly a little disconcerting.

But it's his eyes that do it. Stunningly, brilliantly blue, the aquamarine of the ocean on a clear, sunny day. My absolute favorite color in the world because that's the color of the sea on a perfect dive. Virtually all of my favorite memories are attached to that color.

And we're standing really close together. More like slammed together, really; our bodies still touch from head-to-toe. My eyes drop to the chest a couple inches from my nose. God, he's sculpted. Not in an overdone way, but enough to show he obviously takes care of himself. Probably all the diving.

The chest expands in a sharp breath. My gaze snaps back to those eyes.

"Who are you?" he asks with such an air of authority I finally figure it out.

"Oh, you're Tate, right? Hey, I'm Pippa," I say, smiling.

He stares at me, and then takes one very large, one very obvious step back.

"Oh, whoops," I laugh and take a step back myself. "Again, my bad. Didn't mean to walk into you; I was looking at the vessel and wasn't paying attention to where I was going."

"You might want to stop doing that, then, if you're going to be aboard a ship for three weeks."

"E-excuse me?" I say, taken aback by the blatant rudeness.

"Again, who are you, and what are you doing on this ship?"

Okay, so is this guy an asshole, or what? I already apologized. I'd respond if he'd give me a second to do so. I blink at him, taking him in again without the color of surprise to distract me.

He wears linen shorts and shirt, both heavily wrinkled, the shirt half-unbuttoned. Many hours under the hot sun have tanned his skin to a deep bronze, which contrasts starkly with his white clothing. He wears it negligently, and despite its disheveled appearance, I can still tell it's expensive.

My stomach twists in a sinking feeling. The disdain he's directing toward me is completely unwarranted. What is the *matter* with asshole men today? Have they all decided to unfairly bitch me out for things I haven't done?

This look is even worse than the hostel owner's anger. It's the one someone gives you when you're hopelessly in the way, and of no possible use to the person who's just *too* important to have to deal with your ineptitude.

"I'm the steward," I say flatly.

His gaze narrows. "No, you're not. I was there when she was hired."

"Well, she didn't show up, so you're stuck with me."

His head jerks back like he can't believe I'd speak to him that way. Well, he'd better get used to it. I might be the help, but I'm not a doormat. I don't mind apologizing when I've messed up, but his overreaction to me running into him bodes nothing good for the next few weeks. I'm not going to let him start walking all over me.

"If it's such a problem," I continue, "then take it up with Lachlan. It was his decision. Now, if you'll excuse me, there's work for me to do, and I'd like to get rid of this pack first."

"Just watch where you're going next time," he mutters and pushes past me. I watch him go, shocked that such a troll could be given control over this huge vessel. If this is who Lachlan associates with, then maybe I should be wary around him after all because Tate is clearly no sterling example of an upstanding character.

I've dealt with men like Tate before. Oh yes. There's no one my parents would love more for me to marry and pop out a couple of kids with than an I'm-so-stupidly-wealthy-I-get-to-call-diving-for-treasure-a-real-job kind of man. There have been many of them over the years my parents have pushed in front of me, and every one of them were utter assholes.

Who knows if I even *want* marriage and kids, and at nearly thirty-one, that's probably how my life is going to go. I've had more meaningful life experiences traveling the world since I graduated high school than most people would have in three lifetimes. I'm immensely proud of that, even though it means potentially sacrificing having a "normal" family.

None of my experiences would have happened if, after graduation, I'd promptly shipped myself off to the Ivy League in order to find the most eligible heir on campus.

That life isn't for me, and *this* guy is a Grade-A symbol of everything I loathe about it. No matter how beautiful his eyes might be or how much I want to run my fingers through his tousled hair, that's not going to change. He's bad news.

So, yeah, he's the most beautiful man I've ever seen.

But I don't think I could hate him more.

CHAPTER FOUR

SCHILLER

"Dude, what in the fuck is wrong with you?"

"What are you talking about?" I growl.

I feel more than see Bentley roll his eyes. "Schill, since this afternoon, you have been an absolute nightmare to be around. I get you don't want to be on this boat, but weren't you the one who took the job anyway? You could have just refused. We could be in a five-star villa right now, surrounded by beautiful women and plenty of booze.

"If you're going to force me to gallivant across the ocean searching for a wreck you and I both know we are never going to find, at least don't be a fucking dick while you do it. It's only the first night, for fuck's sake. If you're like this now, what the hell are you going to be like at the end of three weeks?"

"I'm just hungry," I say, which is only half a lie. It's true I haven't eaten in hours but unfortunately, I find myself gripped by hunger of a different kind.

Hunger I hadn't known existed until a few brief moments in a hallway.

Bentley snorts. "Sure, man. Whatever you say."

I let it go, hoping he'll drop it. The last thing I want is to send him in the right direction by telling him what really has me tied up in knots. Or rather, *who*. Bentley doesn't know about the green-eyed beauty. Not yet. And when he does all hell is going to break loose, because that woman is available—I damn-well checked her left hand—and my friend is an absolute shark.

Furthermore, she's exactly his type. Not in looks. Oh, no. Bentley doesn't have any physical preferences when it comes to women. He'll fuck anything. If they're alive and breathing, that's enough for him. But what does matter is whether he can get them to do whatever he wants.

The women think they're manipulating *him* into giving them pretty clothes or whatever else they want, and all the while, he's manipulating *them* into giving him plenty of head. A couple of nice outfits and a pretty handbag are pittances for a man like Bentley. Out-of-this-world blowjobs, on the other hand, not so much.

It's rather hypocritical of me to find it so disgusting since I used to do it myself, but I like to believe I grew out of it. Bentley still sees no problem with the arrangement.

"Gentlemen, ready for dinner after a hard day's work?"

Lachlan enters the salon, clad in yet another linen suit. It took me a few hours, but I figured out how he keeps his linen so wrinkle-free—he changes practically every hour. A truly annoying affectation, but unfortunately, I've seen worse.

"We haven't done much work," I say, "seeing as how we got underway only a few hours ago."

Lachlan drops down into the seat on the other side of the dining table. He wipes invisible crumbs off the obviously immaculate tablecloth before him.

"Anal," Bentley whispers.

My lips twitch, but I fight back the smile. Antagonizing my new boss won't help the situation. And I need to get close to him if I'm going to accomplish the real reason why I accepted this job.

Lachlan sends us a lazy smile, as if guessing what we're discussing. "Work? I suppose you're right. That's what the staff is for, yes? By all means, I want you to enjoy yourself during your time on my ship. Leave the real work to the employees."

Made was right. This guy's a dick, as well as something else, something vaguely sinister that I don't want to overanalyze as it will oblige me to do something about it. I have no desire to discover whatever it is he's involved with; I want to sabotage his ability to find this wreck and then send him on his way, disappointed but no hundred million dollars richer.

Even Bentley's subdued at Lachlan's words. Bentley throws his money around in truly unimaginable amounts, but he always tips well, and his entire staff is salaried with benefits. It's the one thing we readily agree on—if I still had a staff, that is.

"Are you ready for dinner?"

My gaze flicks to her. I've spent the afternoon convincing myself my reaction to her was merely in the moment, but one look at that face proves how much I deluded myself. My fist clenches around my glass as she stalks into the room, multiple dinner plates in hand.

"Why, yes, lovey, we are," says Lachlan, smiling at her in a way that can only be deemed predatory.

"Well, then, the owner first, of course. I hope you built up an appetite," she says, smiling suggestively at Lachlan before placing a plate before him.

"Perhaps you should join us," Lachlan muses, leaning over a bit to stare at her ass while she comes around the table to place the other plates in front of Bentley and me.

"Oh, but I couldn't; I'm here to work," she says on the way back out of the room.

But she sends Lachlan a wink over her shoulder just before shutting the door behind her.

My mood sours. If I'd need any further proof to convince my dick exactly why my first instincts about her were correct, that little interaction was fucking stellar evidence. Bentley and I might as well have not even existed. Oh, no. Not in front of the affluent Lachlan.

When we were alone, however, with no other eligible men around to realize she's playing them as well? Yeah, then she had zero problem flirting with me.

If there's anything I realized about our little encounter in the hall, it's that the blonde—Pippa, even her fucking *name* is cute—is exactly the kind of woman to play every side until she finds her next beau. Some poor sap just tripping over himself to be her next plaything.

I mean, for fuck's sake, earlier in the hall I didn't even know she *existed,* and she's all "Ohhh you're Tate? Heyyyy." like she knows me, all while batting those insanely sexy green eyes at me.

Of course she figured out who I am. Like all vultures, she knows her prey, or perhaps she's a shark—the female kind—and smells blood in the water. Did she worm her way on board because of who Lachlan is or who I am? Or hell, who Bentley is, for that matter? How she found out is beyond me, but it only means one thing.

The number of women who've thrown themselves at me because of my money would make me wealthy a second time over.

Does this chick even know how many other women have tried to engineer such a trick with me? The ol' oops-so-silly-of-me-I-didn't-see-you-there gag. Even the wife from last week tried it! They think if they literally run into you, you're liable to just fall down at their feet and let them lead you around by the nose. I've long since been able to see through such tactics; now they just piss me off.

And it's not like they actually care. It's not even like they're actually attracted to me, damn it! They just know I'll inherit an insane amount of money from my family, so I'm ripe for the taking.

When I was a younger man, I took advantage of it. Sure. But that was then, when I was young and stupid, and thought I could buy love with money, massive hotel suites, and two-thousand-dollar bottles of champagne. I'm not proud of it, of course, but that was a long time ago, and now I'm far too jaded to see it for anything but what it is: pure desperation. On her part, but also on that of any man who agrees to it.

I rarely have any interaction with the fairer sex now, not when they inevitably discover I could never work another day in my life and still be very comfortable indeed. I dress like a bum and act like one too, and to everyone in this hemisphere, a bum is what I am. One who can dive pretty damn well, admittedly, and one who knows more about a sunken treasure ship than anyone else, but a bum still the same.

Now she shows up, acting like the rest of them.

It wouldn't be so irritating if she weren't so incredibly beautiful. When she lifted her face to mine after walking into me, I actually forgot how to breathe. How is a woman that naturally gorgeous? She'd been wearing ratty clothes, not a speck of makeup, and had hair tumbling out of a messy ponytail. I wanted to plow my hands into those blonde curls, shove her up against the wall and take her mouth with mine, damn it. It's been years since I've been so instantly attracted to a woman.

For it to be for a brainless gold digger pisses me off.

Then her gaze dropped to my chest, allowing me to drag air into my lungs and take control of the situation. Or at least try to, that is, until she yelled back at me for being a dick. I won't deny I was rude to her, but it's not like she can talk, since all she cares about is getting ahold of my assets.

Better to cut off the attempt before it happens and spare us all the trouble.

But that means I have to sit here and stare at her through dinner without being able to do a damn thing about the attraction.

She's wearing a uniform like the rest of the staff, but on her it looks obscene. Not because she's particularly curvy; in fact, she's on the slim side, graceful, but so tall that the skirt hits her much higher on the thigh than it would on other women, making visible miles and miles of fucking stellar legs.

"Oh, I see," says Bentley, glancing from me to her. "You like Pippa."

My eyes snap to his. "You know her?"

"Of course."

"Of course," I say sarcastically. "I should have known you'd sniff her out immediately."

Bentley's eyes narrow. "Unlike you, I was actually present when Lachlan presented the staff. Where were you, by the way? How did *you* meet her?"

Bentley laughs when I refrain from telling him. "So, you calling dibs, then?"

I glare at him.

Bentley smiles, and it's a little feral. "This is the part where you argue with yourself between saying she's not a toy to be fought over and telling your friend to piss off from what you saw first, right?"

"Fuck you."

He snorts. "I'll take that as a yes. I gotta say, though. You're not usually one to go for the dumb gold diggers."

"That's a rude thing to call someone," I growl, regardless of the fact that I literally just thought that about her myself. Besides, her comeback in the hall was just a little too quick for her to actually be stupid.

Bentley considers me for a long moment, sloshing the bourbon around in his glass. "Hmm."

"Don't 'hmm' me. I just don't want any extra drama. There's already plenty enough on this boat as it is."

Bentley takes a sip from his glass, his gaze flicking over my shoulder. I turn in time to see Pippa returning with the next course; she places everyone's down and then comes around with mine. She stops directly behind my chair and leans over, placing my plate directly in front of me. Her scent, the smells of salt and summer air and soft woman, slams into me, and I go rigid.

"Enjoy your dessert," she says, and although she speaks to the room at large, her husky voice is mocking enough that tells me she's addressing me alone. And that the *last* thing she wants is for me to enjoy this fucking dessert.

"Thank you," I mumble, shifting uncomfortably in my chair. If she continues standing behind me like that, I'm going to get hard right here in this chair, and then she really will hate me.

"You're so welcome," she says sweetly, her low voice making my stomach clench. Women shouldn't have voices like that, for fuck's sake. She sounds like she's just rolled out of bed after having sucked my cock dry.

"Is there anything else I can get anyone?"

I can think of about five X-rated things right off the top of my head.

Lachlan smiles at her silkily. "That's all for now, lovey, but if that changes, I'll be the first to let you know."

My gut clenches again, this time for quite another reason. He's staring at her with the kind of predatory interest that gets a man punched by another. I suck in a deep breath, careful not to move; between Lachlan and the woman behind me, my control is hanging by a thread. If it snaps, I'm not sure whether I'll beat his ass or take her right here in front of everyone.

"Enjoy, then," Pippa says and leaves. I don't dare look over my shoulder to watch her go, but I can actually feel it when her presence leaves me. I cut into my course with a calm I don't feel, ignoring the look my friend sends me.

When I finally glance up, Bentley chuckles and whispers, "You say you don't want any more drama, Schill, but the thing is, I think it's already found you."

CHAPTER FIVE

SCHILLER

E verything goes fine until the fifth day.

We head out into the Bali Sea, past the islands of Nusa Penida and Lombok, and into open water, straight for where many expeditions have searched for years to find the *Galvanizer*. During the day, I lead one dive in the morning and another in the afternoon, letting the crew linger over lunch long enough that the nitrogen has left our bodies before diving once more.

At night, I avoid her.

That's not possible during dinner; her entire job consists of feeding us and making us comfortable after an exhausting day diving. Proper manners dictate I attend such meals, where I'm subjected to more views of those impossibly long legs and Bentley snickering at me.

I'd prefer to eat in my own quarters, but Lachlan nixes that idea from the beginning, insisting on hearing every last inconsequential detail about the dives and whether I believe we'll find the wreck soon. Which, if I have anything to say about it, we won't.

So instead, I sneak looks at the legs and hope this rich idiot gets tired of his pet project early, so we can head back to port, and I can escape off this yacht.

It doesn't happen.

Four days drag by; the only time Pippa speaks directly to me is on the second day when she asks whether she might join us on one of the dives. I shoot her down immediately; I have neither the time nor the inclination to babysit. Most of our attempts are nearly eighty feet deep, well inside the range of advanced diving. I can't afford to ensure that she's okay while we're operating heavy and dangerous equipment. Every man on this team has been carefully selected to complement the rest. There's no room for anyone else, and this is not a recreational charter.

After that, her demeanor becomes even cooler toward me. Nothing, in particular, would make one suspect she dislikes me; Pippa offers to re-serve me coffee just as often as the others and ensures my meals are just as hot as everyone else's. But our exchanges are barely civil "Would you like another dessert?" and "No, thank you." Bentley gives me shit about it at every turn.

And then on the fifth day, it all goes to hell.

"Tate!" a voice cries from the deck.

"What now?" I mutter, grabbing my water bottle and storming out of my cabin, where I'd been resting after the morning dive. I no longer recover between dives out on deck, not when it means suffering her scorn or my friend's teasing.

"What is it?" I ask as I hit the deck, but then swear as the answer becomes obvious. "Christ, Falon, what the hell happened?"

One of our divers is sprawled on the floor, blood gushing from his leg as the rest of the crew helps him stop the bleeding. He shrugs. "Slipped on the wet deck by the stern and went down on the dive knife I was stowing. Sliced it right open."

We all wince. Jesus.

"It looks worse than it is. The medic aboard will sew him up," Made says quietly beside me, "but he's not going to be able to dive."

I plow a hand through my hair. I'm glad the guy's going to be okay, but now what? Sure, one of the other guys could take over the camera for Falon, but I assigned him the role of photographer specifically because he was the least qualified out of the bunch. The others have more important, more dangerous tasks to perform, like excavation around the wreck sites and operating the lift bags. So unless Lachlan is willing to forego documenting the trip—unlikely, since he's out for glory—then that only means one thing.

We're going to have to turn around, and we're already almost a week from shore. It'll take days to get back, hire someone new, and then turn around again. At that rate, this trip could turn into over a month-long expedition. I have no desire to let that happen.

"All right," I say, "let's get him to the medic."

One of the other divers asks, "What are we—"

"I don't know," I mutter, plowing a hand through my hair.

"What's going on here?"

We pause in lifting Falon from the deck. Lachlan stands before us, a pissed look on his face. The other divers glance at me. This is very much the Lachlan show, and they, being locals, are far too worried about getting fired to push back.

"Just a simple accident," I say. "We'll take care of it, but he can't dive. Unless you're okay with proceeding without a photographer, we'll need to return to—"

"Absolutely not."

"Lachlan," I say through gritted teeth. "Look at him. The man is injured. He can't possibly dive safely."

Lachlan waves his hand as if he can't be bothered. Which, of course, he can't. "I'm aware of that. Just dive without him."

"Well, we could," I say slowly, "but it would really be better not to. We're short a man and—"

"I'll do it."

Pippa steps out from behind the bar where she's been serving post-dive refreshments.

"That's not necessary," I begin, but Pippa ignores me entirely and turns to Lachlan.

"You'll remember, sir, the reason you hired me in the first place was because I can also dive. Looks like you need me, after all."

You need me after all.

A strange electricity zaps through me, an awful kind of foreboding I'd do well to remember. I don't need her. At all. And what I *really* don't need is someone trying to interfere with my dive team.

"That's kind of you to offer," I say, glaring at her, "but it would be better to—"

"What are you talking about, Tate?" Lachlan says. "You just said you're down a man. Here is another man. Well, woman. And a very nice one at that. Why not take advantage of her? It's settled. I expect a report on this afternoon's dive as soon as you're finished."

Without another word, he heads back inside, leaving the wreckage of his command in his wake.

Pippa flashes a smile at me, not even attempting to hide the fact she's gloating. Bentley winks and salutes me mockingly from his deck chair with his half-consumed drink. The other divers glance from Pippa to me; they've dived with me for nearly a week now and know I'm an absolute stickler about keeping to the agreed-upon dive plans. It's not because I'm an asshole, although I'll be the first to admit I can act like it.

It's about safety. Divers *die* when they deviate from the plan. There is zero room for mistakes that far beneath the surface. Get caught in commercial fishing line too thin to see with the naked eye? You die. Run out of air? You die. Get separated from the rest of the group? You die. Stay down too long and not have enough air for a mandatory decompression stop? That's right. You die.

There are consequences for making a mistake during a dive. It's not like other sports, where you can mess up and learn for next time. With diving, there *is* no next time.

I've never lost a man on a dive before, and I sure as fuck am not going to start now. Divers are trained to call the dive when something goes wrong. You don't push through it and continue on bravery alone. You *stop*.

I wouldn't expect Lachlan to know any of that; he's not a diver and doesn't know the risks. That's why he hired me. It's my entire job to prevent shit like this from happening. And as much as I don't want to find the *Galvanizer*, I still intend to keep my men safe.

But *she* knows that safe divers end an expedition if there's a man down. Well, if she's the great diver she keeps saying she is then she should know that. So if she's not lying, then that means she deliberately inserted herself into the discussion because she knew Lachlan would agree to it even though it would piss me off.

And she was right. I'm pissed as hell right now.

"Can I speak with you, please?" I say, trying to keep the anger out of my voice and obviously failing because the rest of the group drop their gazes back to Falon's injury.

"Of course."

Pippa follows me as I stalk inside. I rip open the door to the public head and motion her inside.

"The bathroom? Really?"

"I don't want you in my cabin, and your room isn't private. Where else won't we be overheard?"

She rolls her eyes, but steps inside. "I really wouldn't care if someone heard us; we're not sworn to secrecy."

"I'd mind," I mutter darkly, slamming the door shut behind us.

Pippa glances in the mirror and then turns to face me, folding her arms across her chest. A brow raises in challenge. "Well?"

"You deliberately went over my head out there."

"Yep."

I blink. "And you admit it? Just like that?"

She shrugs. "You needed another diver and were too bull-headed to utilize the obvious resource."

"I'm not bull-headed," I say, jaws clenched.

"Could have fooled me."

"Look, I get that you have your own gear, but I'm not bringing some amateur diver down there when we've already had one injury so far."

"I'm a certified master diver!"

"They hand those cards out like candy, and you know it."

Her mouth thins in a mutinous line.

I continue, "This is *my* expedition. Lachlan might be bankrolling it, but I'm the one running the show. I won't tolerate someone not following my orders. You fucked up."

Her head rears back. "Your orders? This isn't the Navy, Tate."

I ignore what hearing my name on her lips does to me. "This is about safety."

"This is about your ego."

"Having an untested diver in the water is dangerous!"

"Oh, and being down a man isn't?"

She has me there. "It's still not an acceptable risk. I was going to convince him to return to shore when you butted in! We could have been underway by now if you hadn't interfered."

Her eyes narrow. "Why are you so resistant? That would add weeks to this endeavor. Don't you *want* to find the wreck?"

Like I'm going to tell her my real intention is to sabotage finding this wreck. "What I want is a safe atmosphere for my divers. No damn treasure is worth someone getting hurt. Don't *you* want to keep people safe?"

"So get me in the water!" she says in exasperation. "Take the afternoon off from your oh-so-important treasure hunt to make sure I can handle myself. It's not like Lachlan's going to know the difference, anyway."

I glare at her, jaws clenching. She's not wrong. In fact, she's entirely right. We're not going as deep this second time, anyway. The water is mostly clear here.

"Fine. Get your gear and after the rest of my surface interval, I'll see whether you're talking out your ass."

"Yeah, you're going to have to cut that arrogant shit right now," she snaps. "No one should get in the water with someone they want to throttle. Leads to fuck-ups, as you well know. Or are you only picking and choosing which safety rules you'd like to abide by on this little trip?"

"If I determine you can hack it after the dive," I growl, "then I can be pissed later, because then I'll *really* know you should know better than to change a dive plan on the fly to make up for something going wrong. Accidents mean cancelling the rest of the trip. But because you said you can do it, now Lachlan won't listen to reason."

She gets right in my face, eyes lit with fury. Since she's so tall, it's not even that hard for her to do. She just goes up on her toes and sneers at me virtually eye-to-eye, her face flushed and chest heaving.

It's so magnificent my breath catches. Again. That's twice now she's surprised such a reaction out of me. I want to bend her over the sink and drive into her until she's flushed for an entirely different reason. The mental picture of it springs to life with such sudden clarity that I barely hold back a groan.

"Let's get something very straight," she hisses. "You and I both know I can dive perfectly fine. If you didn't truly believe that, you wouldn't even let me get in the water in the first place. What this is really about is that you have some problem with me. You think I'm a bimbo out to steal your precious money, if what Bentley says is true about your bullshit behavior. Which he's reiterated. Multiple times, in fact. Newsflash: I don't give a shit if you're inheriting the moon itself. Not interested."

"That's not the problem," I snarl.

She scoffs. "Oh, yeah? Then enlighten me."

I crowd her into the sink, caging her with my fists slammed down on either side of her slender waist. Her eyes go wide, and that mouth drops wide open in shock.

"The problem is that even with you spitting in my face I

still want to fuck you so hard I can barely control myself. And here's a newsflash for *you*, lady: I don't *want* this urge to take you right here on this damn sink."

And then I shove out of the bathroom, leaving her still gaping at me.

CHAPTER SIX

PIPPA

W ho the hell does he think he is, ordering me around like that? He's not my employer, Lachlan is. Sure, if I end up diving for him, then I'll need to follow his directives, but the way in which he goes about it—his incessant arrogance—is exactly like that of every other man my parents have tried pushing on me on the few occasions I've visited in the last decade.

And then there's the other thing.

But I'm not going to think about *that*. No way. Definitely not. I certainly won't contemplate the way his voice rasped as he growled that he wanted to fuck me. Nor will I be remembering the wild look in his eyes as he said it. And if the sensation of his hard body crushed against mine somehow pops into my head, well, I'm just going to ignore that, too.

What kind of man *says* something like that to a woman?

Oh, right. An arrogant asshole used to getting his way. And damn me if it didn't make me throb with desire.

Well, fine. So I'm attracted to the dick. And, apparently, he's attracted to me, too. That's just chemistry. Whatever. Plenty of people are attracted to each other all the time without acting on it.

Because there will be no giving in to the attraction. My body might lust for him, but my mind knows better, and in the end, my head always wins out. Tate clearly dislikes being attracted to me also. Great. We can both keep resolutely ignoring it and get on with this trip.

And if I have to remind myself of that a few times before it sticks, then so be it.

Resolved not to lose my head over a man, I throw open the bathroom door and practically run right into Made, who's standing in the hallway right outside the head.

"Oh, sorry, Made. Do you need the—"

"Did Schiller convince you not to dive?"

I blink at him. "Tate? Well, I mean he tried."

Made's expression flattens. "But you insisted."

I fold my arms over my chest. "Is there a particular reason I shouldn't get in the water? Do I seem like someone who can't handle it?"

Made casts a glance out the cabin window, studying the ocean instead of replying. Finally, he returns his attention to me.

"My father wanted me to look out for you, yes?"

My hands drop to my sides. "Yeah ..."

Made makes a frustrated gesture. "It would perhaps be

best not to ... put yourself in front of Lachlan any more than you have to. Okay?"

"And diving would do that?"

He gesticulates again. "Possibly. Lachlan is just very committed to finding this wreck, which no one has ever found even a hint of, and he's known to have quite a temper when he's disappointed. It would probably be better for you to stay out of the potential line of fire. Lachlan can be ... unstable."

"Does Tate know?" I ask in alarm, despite my vow two seconds before to ignore the man completely.

Made shrugs. "He has his own reasons for being here."

"And what are those?"

"This wreck affects him personally."

"How so?"

Made startles as if he's said too much. "I mean that Bentley told me he's been trying to find the wreck himself most of his adult life. Has staked his personal reputation on it, in a way. That's all.

"Unfortunately, I suspect that in the unlikely event he actually *does* find the wreck, his idea on what to do with it is going to differ wildly from what Lachlan will want. But you know Tate—"

"I'm really beginning to," I say dryly.

He gives me a considering look. "Perhaps. Anyway, you know a man like Tate is not going to just go along with whatever Lachlan wants. The rest of the crew—even me—sure. We need these jobs. But Schiller can do whatever he wants. He's got the affluence and reputation to do it."

"I had a chance to get to know him on our previous excursion. It doesn't seem like it, but he's a good man. Surly, but inherently good. He'll butt heads with absolutely anyone if he believes he's right. Something I suspect you've already experienced yourself. That's just not a good combo in this situation."

"Do you think he's in danger?"

Made stares at me for a long time. "No. I don't think so. Anyway, the point I'm making is that I want to honor my father's wish to watch out for you, and this is me doing it. Consider staying out of the picture. It's hard to become furious with the woman who serves the meals."

I stare at the floor in thought. Well, hell. Is this the real reason Tate's been such an asshole? Maybe it wasn't really about me to begin with. Or maybe it was, but he was already pissed off for whatever reason, and I just sent him over the edge. Not that any of this is my fault, but it is interesting. Who knows why this wreck is so personal to Tate? There appears to be more forces at play here than I originally thought.

I should stop antagonizing the guy. His being a dick to me is unacceptable, but some people just can't handle stressful situations without lashing out. If he continues his bullshit with me, I'll call him on it, but I'm not going to go out of my way to goad him, either.

Especially not with the bathroom interlude bubbling between us now.

"Being down a diver won't exactly help this situation," I finally say, quietly.

"No," Made admits just as softly.

I sigh. "Then the right thing for me to do would be to help however I can."

Made's shoulders slump. "I was afraid you'd say that."

"That's because it's true."

He sighs, too. "Yeah. It is."

"How about this?" I say. "We'll be dive buddies. Tate's certainly not going to want to be mine. It'll be perfect; you can still keep your dad's wish by watching out for me—and I can keep mine to him about you, too, I guess."

Made smiles, but it doesn't quite reach his eyes. "Sounds like a plan."

Made follows me out onto the deck; he helps gather my dive gear and assemble it, carefully checking each instrument before handing it to me. While I can do it myself, and even will after he does—a diver always checks her gear—it's nice to have someone fuss over me. I honestly can't recall the last time that's happened; most buddy checks on dives end up being perfunctory at best.

Tate comes over with his own gear just as I finish assembling mine. He flicks a glance at my pony bottle, then at me, but unlike Made, the fact that he doesn't acknowledge it, likely means his belief that I'm a shitty diver is utter bullshit.

The rest of the dive team assembles around us as Tate places his tank on the deck next to mine and says, "Okay, then. We're going to do two dives with a surface interval of forty-five minutes in between. First dive to a depth of sixty feet, with a bottom time of forty minutes before ascending.

Second dive will be to forty, with a bottom time of thirty minutes. Safety stops of three minutes at eighteen feet for each dive. Sound good?"

I pull out my dive watch and do a quick consult. My computer will automatically calculate the safety stops and rates of ascension and descension for me, but I prefer to do the calculations myself as well, instead of putting my life in the hands of an electronic device.

"That should be fine. We're well inside the safe parameters for both dives. Have you included the residual time from your dive this morning into those calculations?"

"Do you really need to ask that?"

I shrug. I'm not going to leave it to chance. "Is there anything in particular I should know about the dive sites? Currents? Visibility? Landmarks?"

"No current. Viz should be thirty feet clarity, but I'll expect you to stick closer to me than that. We'll be descending along a wall after we reach the anchor, with the usual coral and sea life, but apart from that, no other landmarks."

I nod. "Fine. Shall we?"

He flicks a glance at my pony bottle. "A bail-out shouldn't be necessary; these are conservative dives."

"I don't dive without it," I say firmly.

Tate considers me for a long moment, then shrugs. We don our gear and prepare to enter the water. Made helps, eyes lit with worry. I give him a smile; I've handled many, many dives at these depths, and while my dive partner isn't my favorite, I'm actually excited to get in the water. It's been a few weeks now since my last dive, and I've been itching to get wet. If that means saddling myself with Tate as my dive buddy, then fine.

Once we've entered the water, we signal the boat that we're okay and then head to the bow to descend along the anchor line. Tate signals for us to descend, and I follow him.

And it is so *good* to be diving again. I should have insisted every day until Tate finally caved. The water is absolutely incredible; crystal clear all the way down the anchor line. Tate and I descend hand-over-hand down the line from each side, signaling to each other we're fine once we reach the anchor. Tate signals to follow him and we move to the edge, then drift slowly down over the wall.

Blackness swirls up from below, the impenetrable darkness of the ocean. If a diver's not careful, they will sink and sink and sink hundreds of feet without any hope of surfacing as the pressure of the water forces them down.

But I don't worry about that; I inflate my buoyancy control device enough to arrest my descent once we hit a depth of sixty feet. Our descent has taken barely a minute, and now we have nearly an hour to enjoy the scenery. Checking my air, I signal to Tate I'm ready to continue and he leads me along the wall.

Within seconds I forget he exists.

I love this. I absolutely love it. Some people search their entire lives to find what truly makes them happy, but I was lucky enough to discover it at nineteen years old.

Nothing makes me happier than drifting blissfully tens of feet below the surface. Nothing. The absolute beauty of it is indescribable. Humans don't belong in the ocean; every second we witness it is a privilege. If I could somehow grow gills and live for the rest of my life right here, I'd do it. It's practically nirvana.

A pair of Moorish idol fish dart out from within the coral. My favorite fish! It's a sign, even if they're a common species. I watch, delighted, as the pair circle each other while they flit from coral indentation to coral indentation, their beautiful black and yellow-striped bodies shimmering in the sunlight that has penetrated even this far down.

I turn to Tate to signal about the fish that mate for life, but he's already watching me. I signal to ask if he's okay, to which he responds he's fine, his eyes never leaving mine. There's little I can see of them through his mask, but I'd swear his expression is startled.

Suddenly a shadow falls over us. I glance up, eyes widening at the massive fish above us. Oh my God, it's a Mola mola! I'd been hoping to see one of these on my trip, and here it is, barely ten minutes into my first dive.

Mola mola are skittish fish and one of the most bizarre ones at that. This one is average in size; I estimate it's about six feet long and eight feet tall, its body a rough oval. One fin is perched directly on top of its head, and the other sticks out straight down from its stomach. It's practically two-dimensional, like a flounder. This one probably weighs about two thousand pounds.

I stare, awed, as it drifts along, its long fins fanning furiously to propel its awkwardly shaped body. If a massive dinner plate sprouted fins at noon and six o'clock and then spun along on its rim, it would move almost exactly like this fish does.

Wow. I mean, *wow*. What a delightfully weird creature. Wanting a better view, I make to fall backward so I can drift face-up below the fish as it meanders along the wall, but Tate is just hovering there, barely giving it a glance.

Oh, come *on*, man. Look at that giant fish! Do you not even care? Maybe he's seen enough of them it's no longer interesting, but I'm following this thing. I grab his hand and vault backward, sending both of us onto our backs, tanks down, arms thrown wide like we've just plopped down onto a bed.

We drift, lazily kicking to keep pace with the animal, its giant shadow blanketing us in semi-darkness. And for all its purported shyness and dislike of the bubbles that escape a diver's regulator, this one just keeps swimming along, not caring that we're blatantly following it.

And everything just fades away, the other fish, the fact that I've been robbed, the nightmare of this charter so far, all of it. It's just one infinite moment, where worries and pleasures and life itself just fall away. I'm smiling around my regulator, so happy I could die.

Suddenly, the Mola mola flips over on its side, practically falling on top of us as it dives for the bottom. We freeze and it plummets mere feet from us, drifting down into the dark depths of the ocean.

Ha! That was so cool!

I glance over at Tate, eyes wide like "Can you believe that just happened?!" but he's not even looking where the fish disappeared—he's staring at me. Electricity snaps through me as our eyes collide.

Then his drop down between us. In horror, I realize I'm still holding his hand and *dear God,* my watch says we've been drifting for nearly fifteen minutes. Why the hell didn't he say anything?

I release him immediately; he slowly retracts his hand and then signals for us to continue along the wall. I confirm, following him, still excited from what we just witnessed. Other aquatic life swims past us during the rest of our dive. I point out all the particularly interesting ones to Tate, who merely nods or gives the "okay" sign in acknowledgement.

His gaze weighs heavily on me as we proceed. Seriously, why is he staring so much? I'm easily the least interesting thing down here. He must be one of those divers that's not impressed by marine life, although in my opinion, if you aren't, then why are you even bothering to dive at all?

But he's not impatient about it, at least. He lets me determine our pace, lingering when I linger and swimming on when I see something farther away I'd like to investigate.

Eventually, he signals to turn the dive, and we head back, returning up over the edge of the wall near the anchor line. We ascend slowly, pause for three minutes eighteen feet from the surface to let nitrogen leak out of our bodies, and then make the final ascent to the surface. It's been just over forty minutes, and it made all the bullshit of the last week worth it many times over.

Made is waiting at the ladder when I surface.

"How did it go?" he calls out, a hint of concern in his voice.

"Incredible!" I call back. "We saw a Mola mola."

He grins. "Did you?"

I kick to the ladder, looping an arm through a rung as I remove my fins. Throwing them up to Made, I say, "That thing was huge! I can't believe how weird it looks."

Made snorts, reaching down to steady me as I climb up the ladder. "Was it a big one?"

"Nah, just average. But still, damn! It must have literally weighed a ton. We drifted along with it for a bit, but eventually it had enough of us."

"See anything else interesting, Pip?" calls Falon from his spot on the deck chair they've told him to recuperate in for the rest of the day.

"Just standard stuff," I say, removing the rest of my gear and passing it to Made, who says he'll refill my tank for the next dive. The other divers pepper me with questions in the way that divers do when they want to hear dive stories. Most of them have already done the same dive multiple times by now, but they haven't been pleasure dives, so none of them have been able to see anything particularly cool.

My watch suddenly beeps. I glance at it; the forty-five-minute surface interval is up. Eager to get back in the water, I turn, but Tate is disassembling his gear.

"What are you doing?" I ask. "Don't we have the other dive?"

"That won't be necessary," he says quietly, and then heads inside.

CHAPTER SEVEN

PIPPA

The fighting stops.

Tate doesn't give me any more grief about diving. In fact, he says nothing at all, steers clear of me except to give me orders along with the rest of the crew at the beginning of each dive. We don't discuss the hand-holding incident, or the fact that his eyes never left me underwater.

I'm more than fine with it; between that and the bathroom incident, I know we're walking on thin ice. It was never addressed, obviously, but something tells me Lachlan wouldn't take too kindly to crew members being involved. Even if Tate is somewhere between a crew member and a guest.

And though Tate drops his arrogance toward me virtually overnight and the tension between us eases, he doesn't interact with me, either. It's weird. I got used to trading barbs with the man, and now that it's all stopped, I feel vaguely let down.

His friend, however, finds every opportunity to talk to me. Bentley seems incapable of not flirting with women, but strangely I'm not offended by it, for after each outrageous comment, he sends me a wink, like he knows he's being ridiculous.

I learn that he's also a diver, but when I ask him why he hasn't yet gotten in the water, he shrugs and laughs that letting the full-sized bar go to waste would be a crime against humanity. I'd trade alcohol for diving any day, but I just laugh and shake my head. I can understand just wanting to laze about a boat as nice as this one.

Every meal still has me serving the trio in the stateroom, which kind of sucks since I'm usually tired after a day of diving. But Falon is still recovering; hopefully once his leg isn't as painful, he can sling food at them instead.

Lachlan continues his innuendo, which I continue to pretend to enjoy. Creepy old pervert. As if I'd actually be interested in him. But as Made mentioned, I won't be pissing him off. And to be quite honest, I can tolerate some misogyny if it means getting paid five hundred bucks a day to dive my ass off in one of the most beautiful places in the world.

And I'm definitely doing that. They set me up as the photographer since that was Falon's position, and it's an absolute blast. I've never had the opportunity to use such expensive equipment, and I probably never will again, so I enjoy every moment of it.

Not that there's much to photograph. Well, not much in the way of a sunken treasure ship, that is. Four days pass with nary a hint of a wreck, but there's plenty of cool marine life for me to photograph, which I do shamelessly. Obviously if they actually find the ship, I'll be there to document it all, but what else am I supposed to do in the meantime?

Once the other members of the dive team realize I can shoot pretty well, they start signaling for me to photograph them whenever they're doing something particularly silly in the water. The antics increase until Tate finally snaps.

"Take photos on your own time! If you want to do a third dive after we've finished for the day, fine. Take all the pictures you want then. But when you're down there, I expect you to be working, not using hundred-thousand-dollar equipment as props for photos. I don't want to hear it from Lachlan, got it?"

There's a chorus of grumbled assents from the other guys. Tate happens to be standing between me and them, so I make a big show of taking a bunch of pretend photos behind him. They snicker.

Tate whirls on me. I drop my hands and pretend to be busy doing another safety check of my gear. His fists land on his hips as he says, "That especially means you, Pippa. Stop distracting them, for Christ's sake."

"Tate, you tasked me with documenting the expedition," I say sweetly, ignoring the shiver that rolls through me at the sound of his deep voice growling my name. "That's what I'm doing. As soon as we find sunken treasure, I'll be sure to point my lens at it, okay? What the hell else am I supposed to do otherwise? Just float uselessly with the camera hanging off me?"

His lips twitch, but that sexy—er, no, not sexy—mouth doesn't break out into a smile. I tamp down the sudden disappointment; it occurs to me that I've never seen Tate smile, and before now, that was never a real loss.

Tate steps closer, his broad shoulders practically blocking out the sun as he whispers, "Just cut them some slack, will you? You've already hopelessly distracted them."

"Them or you?" I quip without thinking.

Heat flashes in his eyes. He leans closer, the delicious heat of him making me shiver, "Tread very carefully, Ms. Turner, or I might send you to the brig."

"You wouldn't make me walk the plank instead?"

His lips twitch again. "I'm not a pirate, Pippa."

I laugh outright. "Pity."

He sucks in a sharp breath, then backs away. Over his shoulder, Bentley is wagging his brows suggestively, intensely enjoying our interaction. I give him the finger surreptitiously, and he practically chokes on his mimosa.

"All right, everyone in the water. And at least *try* to take this seriously," Tate adds with an exasperated glance at me.

"You started it," I mouth.

He shakes his head at me. But that mouth fights a smile again. "As you know, we moved during the night, and LiDAR has picked up a potential wreck site eighty feet down. SONAR confirms. It's a bit deeper than we've been diving, so I want all of you to be particularly cautious today.

"This is going to be mostly a recon dive; we'll get the lay of the land and be up without a mandatory deco stop. Total bottom time of twenty-five minutes, got it? Down and back up. Pippa, feel free to skip this one if you don't want to deal with the equipment for such a short dive."

I snort. "It's the first time we actually find a potential wreck, and you want me to stay on the surface? Time to do my job, more like."

Tate is prevented from replying by Lachlan appearing on deck. "So is today the day?"

Tate glances at him. "Unlikely. We've spotted something with LiDAR that could be a wreck and we're going down to investigate."

Lachlan rubs his hands together in pleasure. "And to think I was starting to believe this endeavor would be a giant waste of time. Once you come up, we'll have to celebrate."

"It's unlikely this is it," Tate says quickly. "Understand that. Yes, this wreck isn't currently identified in the system, so it appears to be a virgin wreck, but I don't want you to get your hopes up."

Lachlan smiles. "I suppose we'll have to see, then, won't we?"

Tate makes a noncommittal sound. Made catches my gaze and shakes his head the slightest bit. Isn't this the exact situation he wants to avoid?

The dive team assembles their gear and then enters one after the other. Once we've all signaled we're okay, Tate leads the descent, and we sink down, down, down. I don't mind diving deep, but there are additional concerns that don't pop up in shallow diving.

And this far down, even in the excellent visibility, less light still penetrates, leaving the area murky. Tate signals the direction of the potential wreck, and we move out. I lug the camera equipment along and have to admit Tate was right; it's dark enough that most of the photos aren't going to turn out that great.

Six minutes later, we arrive at what must be the wreck. It's hard to make out much in the gloom; we switch on our flashlights and fan out, spreading around the edges of the structure.

It *could* be the wreck. Everything ages faster underwater, but it's clear this isn't some ship from hundreds of years ago. I search along with everyone else for the name printed across the hull or anything else that would give a clue to its provenance, but come up with little, so I decide my time would be better spent documenting whatever I can. Maybe on the surface my photos will have some important detail that we missed down here. I spend another few minutes shooting while constantly checking my watch; we're going to have to turn the dive soon to ascend within twenty-five minutes.

It happens so quickly I nearly miss it.

I'm panning with my camera, taking a video that we can analyze as well, when a sudden stream of bubbles snags my attention. My head snaps up, searching for the bubbles with my own eyes. There! Air is blasting from Tate's tank; in horror, I realize the O-ring, the rubber seal that prevents pressurized air from escaping, has blown.

At this depth, he'll be out of air in seconds. And also at this depth, if he makes it to the surface on his last remaining breath, he'll have come up so quickly he might get the bends.

A quick glance tells me the rest of the group is on the other side of the wreck. No one but me is getting to him in time. I drop the camera worth tens of thousands of dollars without a thought, already kicking toward him, praying I'll get there in time.

Tate, perpetually cool and arrogantly confident Tate, has begun to panic, an understandable reaction for anyone in his situation.

But panicked divers die.

Instead of looking around for someone to share air with —maybe I was far enough away he thought he was alone— he drops his weight pouches, designed to be cast off in the event of running out of air. The action does what it's meant to do; he shoots for the surface.

Precisely the worst thing to do this deep.

I grab for him, but he's going too fast, and my fingers clasp empty water. And the more he ascends, the less pressure will be holding him down, which means the faster he will ascend with each additional foot. Kicking furiously, I try to catch him, but it's simple physics. I don't reach him.

And now I have a choice to make. Let him ascend and hope we haven't dived long enough that the nitrogen his body has already absorbed won't kill him if he manages to reach the surface without drowning—or drop weight myself and therefore consign myself to potential decompression sickness along with Tate.

As if I could willingly watch someone die.

I drop one weight and inflate my BCD fully, hoping that since I weigh less and am not as muscular as Tate, I'm inherently more buoyant and will be able to catch up to him while still having some weight left to slow our ascent once I do.

I shoot up from the bottom so quickly that pain slams through my skull due to my body's inability to equalize the pressure inside my head with that of the ocean around me. I continue to kick, and yes, I'm finally gaining on him, but we're ascending too fast, so horribly fast. I watch in dread as I ascend ten, fifteen, thirty feet in twenty seconds—a distance that should take sixty to ascend safely. At last, I reach him, my hands latching onto his ankles and yanking down.

Tate, still lost to the throes of panic, actually kicks at my hands in an attempt to free himself. I grip tighter and pull with all of my strength, clawing my way up his body and jerking him around to face me.

All his panicked brain sees when his gaze collides with me is a source of air; he grabs for my own regulator, ripping it out of my mouth. I let him do it; it'll help calm him, and I'm already reaching for my pony bottle, ridiculously relieved I always insist on diving with it. I cram the new regulator in my mouth and clear it. Sweet air rushes into my lungs. If I weren't underwater, I'd sob with relief.

But Tate is still sucking air; he's rapidly blowing through my own tank now as he struggles to regain calm, and we're going to need that air in order to attempt a safe ascent.

I grab his face between my hands and bring him closer, trying to avoid his flailing limbs. His gaze locks with mine, and I signal to him that he's okay, trying to project with all my might that he's safe now. Slowly, achingly slowly, he starts to calm, his limbs slowing and most importantly, so does his breathing. Convinced reason is returning to him, I take one of his hands and wrap it around my chest strap, giving him a concrete task to focus on.

All of this has occurred in the span of seconds, which is great, because we're still ascending way too quickly. Not expecting Tate to be capable of problem-solving at the moment, I take charge of the situation and deflate my BCD. We slow, but right now we need to stop completely and make an emergency mini-safety stop at our current depth to begin letting our bodies off-gas the nitrogen.

So I deflate his BCD as well, hoping that we'll both be buoyant enough to reach the surface. We slow a little more. We haven't fully stopped, but our ascent rate is slow enough now that we'll have to hope it's enough. What we'll do when we reach fifteen feet and need to do another stop when we'll be even more buoyant, I don't know.

Instead, I focus on keeping Tate calm. He's coming around rapidly now, the man I've come to know reasserting himself over the panicked person convinced he was moments from death. We manage to drift up from fifty to forty feet over three minutes, an extra slow ascent.

I check my gauges and glance down; we've probably got enough air to make it to the surface, but it would be nice if we had another tank. Where're Made and all the other divers? They should have realized something was wrong by now and begun to ascend themselves.

I try flashing my light down at them, figuring we've probably ascended too far for them to see the flashes, but nevertheless, I sweep my light in wide arcs in case someone sees. Even if they've already begun ascending, they're still going to be a few minutes behind us if they don't decide to endanger themselves as well to look for us.

Once we reach forty feet, instead of returning to a normal ascent rate to reach the next stop at fifteen feet, I continue to let us drift as slowly as possible in the event that we're too buoyant near the surface to manage a safety stop. I deflate my BCD as it reinflates from the lessening pressure of the water, so we remain as negatively buoyant as possible. Tate comes quietly, eerily placid now, his body crashing from the adrenaline rush. He won't be much help from here to the surface, and I can't exactly blame him. I'm just glad he's not making the situation worse by not following my lead.

As we reach fifteen feet, I happen to notice a shadow nearby. Hoping it's some sort of ledge or reef we can anchor to, I guide us toward it and sure enough, it's the sloped bottom of a cliff. We must have ascended up out of open water and are now approaching a ledge.

I grab onto it, digging a hand into the coral to secure myself. My other hand stays clenched around Tate's chest strap, refusing to let him drift off now that we're this close to the surface. He also secures himself to the outcropping, and in this way, we're able to cheat the forces of buoyancy for a full safety stop, to which I add an additional five minutes to be extra certain we've off-gassed as much of our rapid ascent as possible. We technically weren't down long enough to even incur a safety stop, let alone a decompression stop, but we've got enough air, and now that we have this ledge to hold on to, I'm not taking any chances.

When I'm sure it's safe to continue—as safe as one can be in this situation—I nod to Tate, and we let go. We don't kick; I partially inflate my BCD and let the buoyancy do the work for us. We drift ever upward, taking the last fifteen feet in about half a minute.

We breach the surface, miraculously alive but drifting all alone in the vast ocean.

CHAPTER EIGHT

SCHILLER

She saved my fucking life. *She saved my life.* Just a few days ago, I'd been skeptical she could even dive at all. If she hadn't proven me wrong on that dive—when she utterly entranced me with her pure joy underwater—I would be dead right now. Fucking *dead*.

What the hell even happened? One second I was studying the wreck, and the next all my air just vanished. The O-ring should have been fine. This shit is supposed to be checked by multiple people. For that matter, how did *I* miss it? Was I so distracted I didn't notice a damn faulty O-ring before getting in the water?

Likely. I haven't been able to keep my eyes off her for days, especially whenever we're in the water. A fucking O-ring had been the last thing on my mind.

"Thank you," I croak around my regulator.

"It's fine," she mumbles absently, scanning the horizon.

It's not *fine*. None of this is fine! I just panicked like a complete fucking amateur, and she had to save me. If I'd had half a brain, I should have looked around for someone who could give me air. If she hadn't been around, who knows if I would have made it to the surface. And then if I had, who knows if I would have gotten bent.

I spit out my reg and clutch her tighter around her chest straps. Then I give her a little shake to get her to look at me. "It's not fine. You saved my life. I would have been dead without you. *Thank you.*"

She spits out her reg, too. "Tate, what was I supposed to do, just let you die? Anyone would have done the same."

That's horseshit, and I bet she knows it. "I choked like a fucking amateur," I croak, "and you were there to stop it. You might want to brush that under the rug, but I won't let you."

I pull her closer until our bodies are flush together, our legs tangling as we continue to kick. Pippa sucks in a sharp breath, a faint blush creeping over her cheeks.

"I can never repay you," I whisper against her mouth.

"Y-you don't have to."

"I do," I growl. "I really do. And I can think of a few ways to begin making amends."

"You can?" she squeaks.

My gaze locks on her mouth. Her teeth sink into her bottom lip and I barely bite back a groan. "Yeah," I mutter, my voice hoarse for a different reason now. "But later. We have other things to worry about at the moment."

"Right," she says shakily, leaning back. "The boat."

"The boat."

"I'm going to inflate my surface marker buoy," she says, then busies herself with inflating the neon orange tube. It bobs up and down beside us, a visible marker for any passing boat.

"I've got a beacon," I add. She nods jerkily as I activate it. The boat should catch our GPS location and hopefully will soon be on the way to pick us up.

With nothing else to look at, we stare at each other. Well, I stare at her, and she drops her gaze, before, unable to resist, her eyes dart up to collide with mine again.

"I wonder what happened to everyone else," she says a few minutes later, clearly searching for some topic to distract me from my staring.

Yeah, right; it will be a long while before I'm able to look upon the face of my savior without such gratitude I'm unable to look away. But still, I reply, "Hopefully, they realized something was wrong and returned to the boat."

"Hmm," she mutters, her lips faintly shivering.

"Are you cold?" I ask sharply.

She shrugs. "Adrenaline crash."

"You handled that amazingly well. Fuck, I actually tried to kick you off, didn't I? I'm just remembering that now."

"I mean, I get it."

"That's still unacceptable. You risked your life for me; you could have got bent, too."

"We weren't down long enough—"

"Pippa."

She sighs. "Yeah. I could have got bent, too."

We fall silent then, drifting along. There's fortunately

little current; we shouldn't travel far before the boat finds us. Fifteen minutes pass before Pippa's gaze sharpens on something over my shoulder.

"Over here!" she calls, grabbing her SMB and waving it in the air.

"They have my beacon," I say.

"I know. I just want to get out now."

"Are you feeling okay?" I ask, my hands tightening on her chest straps.

"Yeah. Just beginning to get tired. It's been—" she checks her watch—"God, it hasn't even been an hour since we went down."

"Feels longer."

"Yeah," she says tiredly.

They pull up to us seconds later. People are calling from the deck, so many discordant voices I can't understand a damn thing. I try to get Pippa to go first up the ladder, but she insists on me going, calling up that I need a medical exam, which is damn embarrassing even if it's also necessary.

"Hell, Schill, are you okay?" Bentley says, voice shaken. "What happened? The rest surfaced near the boat, frantic that something had happened to the two of you."

"After we found the camera gear abandoned on the ocean floor, we looked around the wreck for nearly ten minutes before calling it," says Made, pushing through the crowd. "Nearly blew through our no deco stop limit."

They help me onto the deck, removing my gear for me.

I stay sprawled on the floor, neither caring how bad I must look nor wanting to admit the shameful truth.

"The O-ring blew," I say, "I panicked, bolted for the surface."

Bentley winces. He's a recreational diver, likes to dive the pretty but unchallenging stuff. Even Bent, though, knows doing something so stupid is bad news.

"Out of the way!" the boat's medic yells, shoving through the group to administer oxygen.

"God, no," I say, batting it away. "I'm fine."

"You surfaced eighty feet on one breath, and you're refusing oxygen? You're lucky you're not dead," the medic snaps, shoving the oxygen mask in my face.

I bat it away again. The medic makes a face and begins checking my vitals. "I'm *fine*. I would tell you if I thought there was a risk. What you're worrying about never happened. Pippa stopped me and held me down. If she hadn't been there ... if she hadn't had that damn pony she insists on using ... anyway, she saved my life. Fuck, that's the last time I dive on one tank."

They turn as one to her. Pippa has been quietly disassembling her gear while I get grilled, but at the sound of her name she looks up.

"I took the rescue diver courses like the rest of you," she says quietly, "I did what anyone else would have done."

There's a chorus of mumbled statements disagreeing with this assessment, of which I heartily agree. Pippa might keep insisting that what she did wasn't remarkable, but I know better.

And what I said to her on the surface was no exaggeration. I *will* be showing my appreciation.

"You need to check her, too. She had to go after me to stop the ascent. I must have gone up, what, twenty feet?"

"Thirty," she says, voice still quiet, her head dropped down toward her gear. "In a few seconds. I almost didn't catch you. After you'd dropped weight ... had to do it myself."

My jaws clench, and I say nothing, furious with myself that I endangered another diver with my panic. As if sensing the direction of my thoughts, Pippa glances up at me and says, her quiet voice loud on the silent deck, "Everyone panics at some point, Tate."

Not *me*.

"What is the meaning of this?"

Lachlan storms onto the deck, likely warned by his captain that something had gone wrong. "Well? Did you find the ship or not?"

"There was an accident," Bentley says. "We're making sure they're okay."

Lachlan's head whips toward his dive crew. "Accident? What the hell happened?"

I'm forced to retell the story, as best I can, dragging answers out of Pippa to get the full picture. Those first few moments are a blur; when Pippa tells the entire story from beginning to end, I'm even more astonished by her quick thinking. Could I have acted that fast? Before today, I might have thought so, but now ...

"What happened to his tank?" Lachlan demands. "What caused it to malfunction?"

"A blown O-ring," I say with dread, suspecting where this might be going.

Lachlan whirls on the group. "Who was responsible for checking the gear?"

And here we go. "That's not—"

"Who was it?"

"It was my responsibility," says Made after a charged moment.

Lachlan swings on him. "You? And what do you have to say for yourself? I'm here to find a wreck, not kill a man! Your incompetence could have put everything in jeopardy. Everything!"

Made says nothing.

Lachlan continues, "We'll be turning around this evening to head back to the island to pick up an associate of mine, and you can be damn sure when we arrive in port, you'll be kicked off the boat!"

"Now listen here," I growl, climbing to my feet. My entire body protests any movement now that it's had a moment of rest. "There's absolutely no reason for that. At the end of the day, it's the diver's responsibility to ensure his gear is safe. It was my fuck-up that caused this. Made had nothing to do with it."

"I don't care."

"Sir," Pippa says, suddenly inserting herself into the conversation. Made's hand flies out to her, as if he would prevent her from speaking, but she only has eyes for Lachlan. "While dive accidents are uncommon, they do happen. Fortunately, I was there to help. But without Made, we wouldn't be able to benefit from his local knowledge of the area. He's dived these waters practically his whole life. We need him while we're still familiarizing ourselves with the area.

"Tate needs his help. If you were to let Made go, we may be delayed for days from finding this ship. We might never find it at all. Is that worth the risk to you?"

Lachlan frowns. He looks from Pippa, who stares back steadily, to Made, who's rigidly standing as if at attention, jaws clenched.

"I could hire another local. And the rest of the crew is local, too," Lachlan says, wavering.

"Yes, but could you guarantee they'd be as qualified? Everyone here is younger than Made. He has more experience. How much time would you lose while anyone new familiarized himself with our mission? Again, something might be missed."

The deck falls silent, everyone waiting to hear Lachlan's reply. We all know exactly what Pippa's doing; there are many qualified people who could replace Made. On a dive island like Bali, they're practically a dime a dozen. I bet even Lachlan knows that. But now she's put the suspicion in his head, and for whatever reason, Lachlan really wants to find this boat. Will he risk it?

"Fine," Lachlan snaps, "but I'm promoting you to directly below Tate. You're now responsible for the safety on this ship. No more serving meals—you'll eat with us. I want reports of all the goings-on on this ship. No excuses. Someone else will have to do your previous job."

"I'll do it," says Made.

Pippa glances at him. "You already—"

"I'll do it," Made says firmly.

"Great," Lachlan snaps. "Now, if we could get underway again? Ms. Turner, I'll expect you at dinner."

I know as well as anyone how badly these locals need these jobs. It's not right that Made has to take shit from Lachlan without defending himself. If I weren't still so damn exhausted, I'd be tempted to lay him out myself. But I suspect Made would be horrified, and it's not my place to interfere in his life. So the reality is, there's two men whose lives Pippa saved today.

CHAPTER NINE

SCHILLER

The rest of the day passes excruciatingly slowly. The medic insists on keeping Pippa and me under observation until dinner, convinced we're going to show signs of decompression sickness. Eventually, however, even he has to admit that isn't going to happen, and he lets us go.

Dinner drags on, Made now serving the group. He doesn't comment on it, of course, but for Bentley, Pippa, and me, there's a definite feeling of discomfort. Lachlan, however, feels nothing of the sort, patently ignoring Made except to accept his plates from him.

He's far too interested in Pippa.

Lachlan asks her so many questions she barely has the opportunity to eat. He wants to know everything about her, from where she grew up, to her schooling, to where she's traveled, to how she became such a competent diver. I want to know the answers myself and listen intently—although I try to hide it. Even Bentley seems mildly interested, which is really saying something, since he's incredibly self-absorbed.

Pippa is cagey about her childhood, but she's more than willing to talk about her travels. With astonishment, I listen as she describes traveling virtually the entire planet and how she started barely out of high school. When I was her age, I'd been heading to Yale, more intent on partying than on actually earning a degree. For all my wealth, no way had I been mature enough then to handle traveling by myself—as much as I would have believed otherwise.

Nevertheless, dinner is excruciating. What I want to do more than anything is ask these questions of Pippa myself, but I'm not going to do so in front of these people, not when I doubt she'd honestly answer. Not to mention I feel strangely compelled to hoard the answers myself.

After dinner ends, I look for her, but she disappears. The events of the day suddenly catch up to me, so I return to my cabin. But sleep proves impossible, those moments underwater flash through my mind over and over. The sickening terror of being convinced I was about to die claws its way up my throat.

I throw back my covers. No way in hell am I getting any sleep soon.

I prowl out onto the deck. I've been trying to sleep for hours and it's completely dark, the only illumination coming from a sole emergency light on deck, a half-moon, and the faint twinkling of stars. I head over to the railing, gripping it tightly as I stare out at the moonlight shimmering on the waves.

It's nearly silent apart from those waves, a faint breeze caressing my face that in this part of the world is hot even in the dead of night. The boat cuts cleanly, silently, through the water and it's incredibly beautiful. Tonight's the first night I've come out here so late; we're usually moving overnight to our next dive site, and so I've never realized how calm it is. It's probably the first peace I've felt since I stepped on board.

We didn't find the *Galvanizer* today. Some other boat, sure, probably a decade younger than the wreck we seek. Who knows what happened to this one. We didn't have time to breach the wreck to search for bodies, and after what happened today, we probably won't. The authorities will have to manage it.

Even worse, all afternoon, Lachlan has been even more rabid about finding the wreck. So far, I've managed to put him off what I suspect is the real trail by suggesting a slightly different direction for us to take, but I wonder at what point my luck will run out. He seems to take my directional suggestions a little less each time I make one.

A scuffling noise sounds from behind me. I whirl around. Pippa is stretched out on one of the deck chairs, staring at me.

"Christ," I say. "You startled me."

"I'm sorry."

"Why didn't you say anything when I came out here?"

She leans back against the chair. "You seemed like you wanted to be alone."

That was true—until I realized she was here. We stare

at each other for a long moment, both of us barely visible in the moonlight. Finally, she nods to the chair next to her.

"Would you like to join me?"

I stalk across the deck to drop into the chair, neither of us acknowledging the significance of her offering the chair and my accepting it.

We lapse into silence, staring up at the star-sprinkled sky.

"It's beautiful, isn't it?" she says a few minutes later.

I grunt in agreement, too focused on the curve of her mouth to give one shit about the sky.

"I've always found it so incredible. No matter where I am in the world, no matter the country, the land, the people, whenever I look up, the sky is always the same—assuming I'm in the same hemisphere, of course. There have been many times in my life where that fact has been an enormous comfort. Do you find that too?"

"Never thought about it," I say roughly, still focused on her mouth.

Pippa keeps her attention on the sky, although she must feel my gaze. "I think the—"

"Are we going to talk about it?"

She finally looks at me. "We've gone over it multiple times today. I know you're grateful. Your thanks were enough. Do we really need to rehash it yet again?"

"That's not what I was talking about," I say quietly.

"Then what did you really mean?"

"Pippa," I say softly. "What else could possibly matter? The hallway that first day. The bathroom."

She inhales slowly, her chest rising and falling. I realize she's also wearing her pajamas, a pair of incredibly short shorts and a thin-strapped shirt. Her braless nipples are tight, jutting out against the fabric of her shirt in the soft breeze. Her naked legs stretch endlessly over the chair, her skin looking so soft I ache to stroke it myself to discover if it really could be that perfect.

Blood rushes from my head, a buzzing sound vibrating in my ears, my cock instantly springing to life. Feeling dizzy, I have to grip the armrests of my chair to keep from picking her right up and straddling her across my waist as I surge up inside her.

A tortured groan must escape me because she falls still. My gaze trails up to discover she's taking in my body, too, her teeth sunk into her lower lip. I want to bite that lip so badly it hurts restraining myself from doing so.

"I've been wondering something," she croaks.

"What?" I ask hoarsely, hoping whatever it is will distract me from this insane urge to take her.

"Made said that you have personal reasons for finding the *Galvanizer*."

Well that fucking worked. My desire evaporates. I lean back against the chair, face tipped up to the sky. "Yeah. Always have."

Pippa doesn't immediately reply, as if searching for the words. "I don't mean to pry, but I've kept wondering if that was part of the reason why you were so, um ..."

"So much of an asshole that first time we met?" I finish

for her, hand scrubbing my face in sudden shame. "I apologize for that. I was a dick to you for no reason."

"I accept your apology," she says quietly. "And, I don't know, I apologize too. I kind of kept egging you on in the days after."

I laugh mirthlessly.

"Do you want to talk about the wreck?"

I shrug. "I don't really talk about it."

She looks back up at the sky. "I understand. But ... we'll go our separate ways soon, and sometimes it's nice to spill your guts to a stranger."

I ignore the sudden twinge of dismay her words elicit and actually consider her offer. I rarely even speak to Bentley about this, although he's known the story for so long it's practically a part of his life, too.

Impulsively, I say, "How much do you know about my family?"

Her head whips toward me in surprise, like she'd accepted I wouldn't take her up on her offer. "Not much, Tate. Bentley told me your family's well-off."

More evidence I misjudged her when we met. Christ, I'm such a dick. I plow my hand through my hair, suddenly embarrassed. "I'm ... my family is *really* well-off."

"I kind of gathered that," she says dryly.

"Sorry," I say, feeling even more embarrassed. "I don't know how else to put that. My family's been involved in shipping for three generations now. Four, if you include me, although I no longer work for them—not that I ever did much.

"I was raised really comfortably. I can admit that. And, though I'm ashamed to admit it, I can also admit that it made me pretty rotten as a kid. My parents were never around, as they were running a company valued at, uh, a few billion dollars."

"Jesus."

I wince. "Yeah ... it's not a small company. You know those giant ocean liners you see piled high with shipping containers? My family owns most of them. Anyway, my parents were never around. I was always expected to follow in the family business. Even gave it a half-assed attempt when I got older."

I sigh and run a hand through my hair. "And?" she prompts, sensing there's more.

"Lawrence Galvan was my godfather."

"*What?*"

"And my parents' partner. Most of my earliest memories are of him. My parents weren't around, but he always found time for me when he occasionally visited. He never married or had kids, and I guess I was his surrogate family. I don't remember much about him since I was so little, but I do remember always being happy when he visited. He was kind of like Santa Claus—rarely around, but when he was it was super fun. He always brought me on his boat, taught me how to swim. All of my earliest memories of being in the water are with him.

"And then when I was five, his ship went down. It devastated me. Hell, it devastated my parents. I don't think they've ever fully recovered from his death—or *disappear-*

ance, as they insist on calling it—but because of it, any chance I had of turning out normal essentially evaporated overnight. You know how Bentley's kind of ... uh ..."

"A rich bitch only caring about superficial bullshit and throwing his money around?"

"He has his good points, too," I say quickly. "But, yeah, pretty much. I was like that as well."

She stares at me. "Really."

I rub the back of my neck, sure that if there was more light on deck, she'd see how red my face has become. "Unfortunately, yeah. Bent and I went to the same schools growing up, both went to Yale—"

"Of course you did."

"—all of it. And we were, I guess you'd say, pretty rowdy all through college and for a few years after."

"You'd say so?"

"Look," I say, growing irritated, "I already said I was ashamed of it."

"You're right," she says quickly. "That was wrong of me."

I sigh. "You're not wrong, though. Anyway, I whored my way through half my twenties, barely putting in any real work at my parents' company, essentially wasting my life and all the blessings I'd been given. That's why I was such a dick to you that first day, by the way. Women used to ... well, they only ever saw the dollar signs behind my name, and when you ran into me, already knowing my name and smiling at me like that ... I thought 'here we go again.'"

"I knew your name because Made had just told me," she says.

"Really? Christ. Of course that's how. Again, sorry for the shitty behavior."

"So what happened next?" Pippa asks after I fall silent, replaying the day we met with new eyes.

I shrug. "And then, one day, I just ... realized what a waste it all was."

"Really?"

I nod. "Bentley and I were at a party. I'd taken a girl with me and we got wasted. Really, really, bombed. And, um, as she was doing yet another line, she looked up at me and said, 'this is as good as it gets, huh?'"

"Wow."

"And I looked at her. And looked at her. And all of a sudden, this voice in the back of my head goes *Really? This is all there is? This is it?* And I just ... freaked out."

"Yikes."

"I dragged myself home. Didn't come out of my room for a week. Just laid in bed, wondering if I'd ever do anything useful, anything meaningful with my life. My parents thought I'd lost it."

"That's horrible."

"Yeah. It was shitty. But all that thinking gave me a purpose, after all."

"The wreck."

"Yeah. I decided to find it. I needed the closure. For myself. My family. Hell, the world. Everyone wants to know what happened to my godfather. They want the treasure, obviously, but I just want to know what happened to him. How he ... died. Whenever someone hires me to find the wreck, I actively lead them away from where I think it might be located after many of my private expeditions. I don't want someone else to find it; only me. Not because of the money, but because I don't want his death to become a spectacle. It's not about the money, but it will be if anyone but me finds it. He was the only person who ever tried to make me a good person. To teach me right. He deserves to be laid to rest with dignity, not as a throwaway line in international news stories about the stupid expensive shit that went down with him."

Pippa stares at me, expression writ with sadness. She reaches out and squeezes my arm. "I'm sorry for your loss, Tate."

I reach over with my opposite hand and squeeze hers. "Thanks, Pippa."

We stay like that for a moment, locked together, then she pulls away, the absence of her hand a terrible loss of comfort.

"I'm kind of in a similar situation."

I do a double take. "Really?"

She snorts, although I can tell it's directed at herself. "The scale is certainly smaller, but yeah. My parents are both physicians. Big time physicians. Dad's a cardiothoracic surgeon, and mom's the head of a hospital in Greenwich. They're the kind of doctors who get flown in to consult on really awful cases."

"I think I can see where this is going."

She smiles wryly. "Yeah. Believe it or not, they're not too thrilled their only child decided to bum around the world instead of having a real career. Or marrying someone with a real career, as my mom would have it. That's why I wasn't nice to *you*, by the way. You reminded me so much of the awful boys my parents pushed on me in high school. The men they've dangled in front of me over the years to try to lure me back permanently. Many of them have that innate confidence, arrogance really, that you do, coming from such affluent situations."

"Hmm," I say, not liking being compared to men she obviously hates. "That must be hard, your parents trying to control your life like that. I can relate."

"Yeah. It was. At first. I finished high school, and they shoved the Ivy League in my face—they wanted me at Yale, too—and I just felt this suffocation, you know? The idea of that life, I just ... I knew it would kill me. Not all at once. But slowly. A little cut there, a bigger one here. Until I'd no longer recognize myself and would be absolutely miserable.

"So one night, a week before my first semester was supposed to start, I snuck out of the house and took a red-eye to South Africa. By the time my parents woke up, it was too late for them to get me back."

"And you've been traveling ever since."

"And I've been traveling ever since. I vowed right there I'd never take a dime from them. And I never have. It was beyond rough at first. The jobs I had to do ... shit, they were awful. But eventually I got certified, and I clawed my way up the levels, and now I can talk my way onto virtually any boat."

"Case in point, this one," I say, a grin stealing over my face.

She smiles, too. "Yep. This one included. And it's definitely turned out to be an interesting one."

"That's a polite way of putting it," I snort. "I don't see how you've put up with me this whole time, let alone Lachlan and even Bentley. You must have hated serving our meals."

Pippa looks at me then, her eyes tracking over my face.

"I think," she says slowly. "I would like to know why you kept staring at me. That first day. With the Mola mola. The whole time, whenever I looked over, your eyes were already on me."

I laugh, the sound low and hoarse. Husky from holding back all the things I want to do to her.

"Why? I'll tell you why." I lean across as far as I can lean without toppling from the chair. "Because, I've never seen a happier human being, is why. Christ, Pippa. You were ... lit from within. I couldn't look away. It was sexy as hell, and from then on, practically all day every day, I've had to watch you like that in the water.

"Just a few weeks ago, I'd never met a woman who enjoys diving as much as I do. Never. And then you come along and completely upend everything. I resisted you getting in the water in the first place because I knew, deep down, I'd never be able to stay away from you then. And I was right. You got in that water with me, and I haven't been able to look away since.

"It's been such damn torture I've had to fuck myself to sleep every night just to be around you. You want to know the *real* reason I almost died today?"

She sucks in a sharp breath, face tipped toward mine. We've leaned toward each other, unable to look away.

"Yes," she whispers. Her tongue darts out and wets her bottom lip. I groan, and she sucks in another harsh breath.

"I was so busy imagining you naked in my cabin that I forgot to check the fucking O-ring. I just fucking *forgot*. Such a basic safety check and it might as well have not existed. My damn training might as well have never existed, for that matter. It's a miracle I've been able to dive around you at all."

Pippa falls still, gaze locked on my mouth.

"Obviously that's not your fault," I growl. "But from the moment you've stepped on this ship, you've pushed and argued and ignored me repeatedly and you've been *right* every fucking time. A man can only resist that for so long."

"Oh," she says. A shiver rolls through her. She's turned on her side, her entire body poised to hear whatever comes out of my mouth next. What that will be, I don't even know. The moonlight falls along the curve of her body, one long, sensuous stroke that has me utterly entranced. I want to slide my hands over that skin, taste the heat of her, suck each sensitive part until she's writhing under me.

My gaze lands on her wrists. They're so tiny, so delicate. Have I ever really noticed how much smaller women's wrists are than mine? Christ, virtually anything could crush them. How was she able to stop me? How did she have the strength to keep her hold as I kicked her? How did she pull me down to her and manage to calm me? I'm not a small man; it's a miracle she managed to save me. I could have killed her along with me in my blind panic.

My attention moves inexorably back to her face, eyes greedily drinking in each delicate line of her features. *This* woman, this incredible creature, is the only reason I'm alive to enjoy the beauty of this quiet night.

"You really are beautiful," I whisper. Her eyes fly to mine. "I think that's what pissed me off about you the most, the first time we met. You were the most gorgeous woman I'd ever seen, and then you opened your mouth, and I couldn't stand you. It fucking ruined it."

She smiles faintly, almost self-deprecatingly. "You know, that's funny."

I still. "Why?"

Her smile grows wicked. "Because it was almost exactly the same for me."

The attraction ignites in an instant. She's reaching for me even as I take her mouth with mine, lunging for her so quickly we both tumble to the deck.

CHAPTER TEN

PIPPA

I fall on top of Tate, my knees straddling him. He breaks our kiss to look up at me, eyes wide as his hands bury themselves in my hair. I stare back, my palms slapped against the deck in the space next to his head.

"Pippa," he groans.

I smile down at him then bite his lower lip. Tate groans again, wrapping his arms around me and tightening until I'm sprawled atop him. He kisses me softly, taking his time, both of us savoring the sensual slide of our tongues against each other. One of his hands slides up to rest over my heart, thumb rubbing in soft circles.

His body is so wonderfully hard beneath me, his skin hot to my touch. My pajamas are so thin there's virtually no barrier between us; I rock against him, and he flinches, then surges up against my core. I trail my hands over his naked chest, glad he apparently sleeps shirtless because now I can finally stroke the incredible torso I've been drooling over for days when he parades around in a swimsuit. His muscles twitch beneath my fingers, his body going taut as I tear my mouth from his and move lower.

"What are you doing?" he rasps, lifting his head a few inches to stare down his body at me.

I remove my mouth from his stomach, grinning at him before pressing another quick kiss to his abs. They clench as he moans, head hitting the deck again as his hips jerk upward.

"What does it look like I'm doing?" I say.

He swallows hard, throws an arm over his eyes. "Here? On the deck?"

"Can you think of a better place?" I slide my hand lower, beneath his waistband, my fingers wrapping around his hard cock and stroking from base to tip.

"Pippa!" he groans, hips thrusting into my hand. "Christ. Someone could ... fuck, that's incredible ... anyone could interrupt us."

The veins in his neck bulge as I continue stroking, memorizing each glorious inch of him with my hand. His skin is so amazingly soft, a delicious contrast to the hardness and barely-controlled strength I know he can give me. Wanting to see him in the moonlight, I inch down his body, pulling his boxers with me until his erect cock breaks free of his underwear.

Beautiful. There's no other word for it. The moonlight illuminates the hard planes of his body, the ridges and valleys of his tightly-wound muscles still cast in shadow. My core throbs with almost painful desire; wetness pools between my thighs.

Tate hisses as the night air hits his cock, his head lifting once more to stare down at me. There's a wildness in his gaze, a kind of startled wonder.

"I don't really care if someone sees us, do you?" I whisper. "Besides it's after midnight. Everyone is sleeping. No one will interrupt us. We can relocate to your cabin if you really want to, but I want you here, now, deep inside me with waves crashing around us and the stars twinkling above. Don't you want that?"

And then I drop my mouth to him.

"Fuck!" Tate croaks. "Oh, God, Pippa." His hands hold my head to him, gently fucking himself with my mouth. I take him deep inside, tongue swirling over his head as he withdraws, which drags a hoarse curse from him. His hips buck upward, thrusting his cock roughly inside my mouth, but he withdraws again before it becomes too much. I moan, sending vibrations down his shaft.

"Pippa, don't," Tate begs, his cock hitting the back of my throat again as he helplessly thrusts up into me once more. "I can't ... I can't take it. I'll come too soon. Oh fuck, that's good. It's too good."

His body is shaking so hard I know it's taking everything in him not to explode. I smile around his cock and moan again. That's perfectly fine with me; I love sucking a man until he's weak from receiving the pleasure I give him.

If that means having to wait for him to recover from the first orgasm I give him, then so be it.

"Damn it, Pippa!" he growls, withdrawing from my mouth and dragging me up his body. "I don't want to come in your mouth. I want to come deep inside your wet, throbbing pussy while I stare into your eyes."

My face is smashed against his heaving chest, his one hand cradling the back of my head while the other slides down my back to slip inside the waistband of my shorts. He palms my ass and then dips lower, finger entering my pussy and stroking deep. I clench around his finger and grind against his cock, sliding it against my clit once and then once again as he adds a second finger to his first.

"Fuck," he pants. "That's still too much."

I lift my head to kiss his chin. "If you come like this, I don't mind. You'll get hard again eventually."

A great shudder rolls through him. He withdraws his fingers. I cry a sound of dismay, but he's dragging me higher up his body.

"First," he growls, "this shirt will have to go. Lift your arms for me."

I comply as he drags my shirt over my head. I gasp, eyes falling shut as the warm air hits my skin. A jolt of heat flashes through me with such force a sudden lassitude enters my limbs. We're really doing this; we're going to fuck right out in the open, our bodies growing slick with sweat from the tropical heat.

When I finally open my eyes and look down, Tate is staring up at me, a mixture of pleasure and restraint on his face. "Your body is so fucking erotic I'm practically coming just looking at you."

I smile slyly, reaching back to stroke him. "I'd like to see that."

He jolts upright, lips capturing one of my breasts. He sucks me into his mouth, tongue circling my nipple as I moan and clutch him tightly to me. I continue stroking him, reveling in the pleasure rocketing through us until suddenly Tate tears his mouth away.

"Stand."

"What?"

"Stand on either side of my shoulders, Pippa," he commands again.

I have no idea what he's talking about, but the wicked look in his eyes tells me I want whatever he's planning. I stand, legs spread wide as I stare down at him. Tate smiles in satisfaction and then begins running his hands up my legs, massaging and stroking and caressing so slowly I'm struggling to breathe by the time he reaches my hips.

"It's time to remove the shorts, Pippa."

I nod silently, still too busy trying to breathe to respond. He grabs the hem of my shorts and pulls them down. I hurriedly step out of them, nearly falling over in my haste.

Tate is staring at my pussy with unabashed need. For the rest of my life, I hope I never forget the look in his eyes.

Tate slides his hands up behind my knees, squeezing tightly. "Kneel over my face, Pippa."

"Oh God," I cry.

His face breaks out in an absolutely filthy smile. "Oh

God is right. You're going to ride my mouth until you're coming against my tongue. Now kneel over me."

I fall to my knees, placing them on either side of his face. Tate's breath caresses my folds, sending a shiver through me. Our eyes are locked together, his hands sliding up to cup my ass.

"Place your palms on the deck above my head," he says.

I do it, leaning over him as the position brings me closer to his mouth. He inhales sharply, fingers twitching on my ass.

"Fuck me," he mutters, eyes locked on my folds. "Arch your back for me."

I arch my back, throwing my head back as well. My eyes drift closed, my arms shaking from the anticipation of what's about to occur.

"Look at me."

Opening my eyes, my gaze drops down to him. We stare at each other, lost in a lust-filled haze until he drags air into his lungs and growls, "Fuck yourself with my mouth, Pippa. And be quiet about it if you don't want anyone to find us."

He crushes me to him.

I gasp, then suck my lower lip into my mouth to keep from crying out. His tongue on me is so perfect, so gloriously hot. Waves of pleasure start building.

He flicks his tongue inside me, stroking deep. I moan, rocking against that tongue, feeling it thrust into me over and over. Using my hands for leverage, I grind myself against his face, my hips circling in tiny circles that have me panting within seconds.

Tate's fingers flex on my ass, drawing me closer, urging me to use his mouth however I need. I writhe against him shamelessly; my head drops down to stare into his eyes. Neither of us can look away. It's just me and those incredible blue eyes shining brightly in the moonlight. And the *need*. The rampant need to come against his mouth overtakes me with such urgency I nearly cry out from it. Only by sinking my teeth into my lip again do I manage not to scream.

Tate's eyes flash with heat, and even with most of his face covered by my pussy, I can still tell it's with satisfied male pride. He knows I'm seconds from exploding and is thrilled it's because of his talented mouth.

He withdraws his tongue and sucks my clit into his mouth. I shatter. My hands fly to his hair, thrusting his head against me as my hips buck wildly. Waves of pleasure crash through me; my head snaps back, my back arching as pure heat explodes out of my core in waves, robbing me completely of all rational thought. Only at the last moment do I manage not to scream with pleasure.

Slowly the orgasm fades. I sag, hands hitting the deck again to keep me from toppling over. With a herculean effort, I lift myself off Tate, my chest heaving.

Tate's hands stroke up and then back down my spine, his hands so large they practically span the entirety of my waist. His mouth's an utter mess, lips and chin smeared with me. It slowly stretches into a satisfied grin.

"That was sexy as hell," he says, voice hoarse.

I'm still struggling to breathe. "That ... I could get used to. Jesus, Tate."

Something flashes in his eyes but it's gone so quickly I almost miss it. I slide back down his body, hands sliding into his hair, fingers massaging his temples as I bring his mouth to mine and kiss the taste of me from him.

"Come inside me now, Tate," I say softly against his lips.

He drags in a shaky breath. "I don't have a condom. Surprisingly, I didn't think to bring one out on deck in the middle of the night."

I push the messy strands of his hair out of his eyes, kissing him lightly again before leaning up a few inches to stare into his eyes.

"I'm on the pill and am tested regularly. It's up to you."

"Up to me?" he croaks."

I drop a kiss to his temple. "Well. More like I've already made my decision. Assuming you're disease-free, of course. Or I could wait here while you go get one from your cabin."

"Not fucking likely," he says, chest heaving. "I got tested last month myself." He grabs my ass again and aligns me over his cock. I watch as his gaze floats down our bodies to where he's poised to enter me. His breath whooshes out in a harsh gasp and then his eyes fly to mine in question.

I smile at him, hands still buried in his hair. His eyes widen slightly, and then slowly, achingly, he works me down onto his cock. At the first inch of him entering me, I sigh, going limp with satisfaction. Tate jerks under me, clearly holding himself back.

"Deeper," I encourage, my face dropping to his chest, my fingers playing in the strands of his hair.

Suddenly, I'm flipped onto my back. "Look at me."

My eyes fly open. Tate's face is inches from mine; his expression twisted in something like desperation. His forearms come down on either side of my head, his biceps bulging. Every inch of his body crushes mine into the deck. Everything about him is shaking. I widen my legs, and in one long thrust, he fills me deeply.

We both moan through closed mouths in the effort to remain quiet. Tate begins thrusting in slow, long pumps that are so perfect I want to sob or scream or both. I wrap my legs around his waist, meeting him with every thrust. We slide against each other for infinitely long minutes, the heat making sweat pour from our bodies. Above Tate's head, the stars are shining down at me, crowning his head in beautiful starlight.

"Oh Tate," I whisper, the pleasure so overwhelming my eyes drift closed as my muscles begin to clench around him. "That's so good. Tate, that's everything."

He begins thrusting faster. "Say my name."

My eyes open in confusion. "Tate?"

"No," he moans, head dropping to the crook between my neck and shoulder. His hips are starting to buck erratically now, his body quivering with his need to orgasm. "My name! Say my name, Pippa."

My hands that had still been tangled in his hair suddenly cradle his head as tenderness rolls through me. I gently lift his head up, waiting for his eyes to meet mine.

"Schiller," I whisper against his mouth, watching the precise instant the sound of his name on my lips sends him over the edge. His mouth crashes down on mine, kissing me desperately as he spills inside me. I take every last thing he gives as my own release barrels through me, the two of us moving together until we're both lying spent on the deck.

CHAPTER ELEVEN

SCHILLER

That night changes everything.

I become addicted; no matter how many times or how many ways I have her, just one look, one smile from Pippa, has me pulling her into a closet or a bathroom or even behind the row of tanks. She spends every night in my cabin; thankfully, her absence in the crew's quarters that must be noticed goes unmentioned.

Even Bentley doesn't bother with his usual teasing, knowing, like I do, that this is not the typical hookup. That an undeniable bond was forged between us that night on deck when I thrust deep inside her and begged her to see me as the man I am and not the name chained to me.

The only person who appears completely unaware that Pippa and I are fucking at every opportunity is Lachlan, but that could be because he's awaiting the apparently unexpected arrival of his business associate, whoever that is. The morning after the dive accident, we turn back for Bali to pick the man up. No matter what I say, Lachlan refuses to finish the dive trip before returning to Bali, saying that his associate is not a man who takes waiting lightly.

So far, I've managed to keep the dives well clear of where all my years of diving have led me to believe the *Galvanizer* likely rests. I'd like to keep it that way. Once we set out once more from Bali, if I'm able to steer Lachlan in a completely different direction, then that will be even better. No fucking way am I letting *this* asshole be the discoverer of my godfather's grave.

Something tells me it might prove difficult, however; each time I suggest altering the route, he grows increasingly irritated. So far he's caved to my suggestions, but unerringly he moves the route back toward where I specifically don't want him to go. Something in the back of my mind wonders whether he might know something I don't, but for now, I'm not pushing it.

It takes a few days to return. It's the weekend, and Lachlan surprises us all by saying that his associate was delayed and therefore won't be arriving until Monday, so we can all take the weekend for ourselves.

Bentley rolls his eyes at me as we step off the yacht after arriving back in Sanur. "I'm assuming you'll be spending forty-eight hours locked in a hotel room with Pippa."

I grin at him. "We may venture out for sex elsewhere."

He frowns. "Just be careful."

My grin fades. "Why?"

"I've just never seen you lose your head over a girl like this in all the years I've known you, is all."

"She's not a girl."

"My point exactly," Bentley sighs. "I'll see you on Monday. I'm going to check into the most expensive hotel on this entire island and spend *my* forty-eight hours lost in the pussy of some beautiful woman myself."

"You don't have to return with me on Monday, you know. You've done more than enough. Singapore awaits."

He snorts. "But I will. Forces are afoot here, and I'm not throwing you to the wolves."

"What?" I say, searching the crowd for Pippa.

Bentley rolls his entire head along with his eyes. "Good God, man. Pull your head out of her cunt for like two seconds. Can't you see Lachlan's worked up about this associate of his?"

My eyes fly to Lachlan, who's staring out at the hustle and bustle of Sanur as if searching for something.

"Hmm," I say. "You might be right."

"I damn well am, and you know it. So yeah, I'll be back on Monday, because whatever that asshole's up to, I don't want you to face it alone. See ya on Monday."

"See you," I say absently, still staring at Lachlan. Perhaps it won't be as easy to misdirect him as I hope.

"So ... are we doing anything this weekend, or should I go find a hostel?"

I turn to Pippa, a wicked smile stealing across my face, Lachlan temporarily forgotten. "Do you actually think I'd let you check into a hostel when I have every intention of fucking you sideways this entire weekend?"

Her face turns faintly red, but she laughs, giving me a

once-over that gets my blood pumping. "Well, I wasn't going to assume. And there *are* ways to hookup in hostels if you're creative."

I prowl toward her. "Is that so?"

She nods.

"Like what?"

She wraps her arms around me. "The showers."

I bring her flush against me. "Really."

"And the locker room, if they have one."

I drop my mouth to her neck, nibbling softly before murmuring against her skin, "How interesting."

"And if they've got an outside bar, you can wait until it becomes dark and then get a little handsy."

"*Really.*"

She laughs. "I mean, that's what I hear. I tend to keep my hookups out of public living spaces."

I pull away and throw an arm over her shoulder. "Well, good, because I have no intention of checking into anything but a place with the biggest bed imaginable."

"If it's all the same to you, can we head up to Ubud? I haven't been able to check out the jungle part of Bali yet, just the beaches."

I press a kiss to her hair. "Sure, Pip. Let me just find a taxi."

"Why don't we just rent a motorbike for the weekend? We don't have a lot of stuff. And then we can explore after we check in. Motorbikes are always the best way to get around."

I lean away far enough to look at her. "You can drive them?"

She winks. "How do you think I got around Mongolia? But because I'm a *really* nice person, I'll even let you drive."

I shake my head. "Christ, you're hot."

Her smile widens. "Well. I may have an ulterior motive. Like getting to put my hands all over you in order to hold on?"

"What a salient point," I say. "Perhaps you should drive after all."

She laughs. "Nice try, Schiller, but I already called it."

Surprised pleasure shoots through me like it always does when she says my name. Since that night on deck, she's taken to calling me by my first name. I didn't have to ask her, would never have made the point to do so, which only makes her doing it mean more to me.

How many times have I wanted to be seen as *me*, and not the son of my parents? Not the heir to the Tate Shipping empire? How many times have women come after me for my money, until I stopped dating entirely? More than I could count.

As if sensing all that, Pippa made the correction of her own volition. I would thank her for it, except doing so would require admitting to feelings I'm not ready to acknowledge to even myself right now.

So instead, I pull her tighter against me, lift her face up to mine and take her mouth in a deep, passionate kiss, not caring about all the people milling around us who start gaping after a few seconds.

When I finally pull away, Pippa smiles dreamily, her eyes still closed. I inhale sharply, pressing another quick kiss to her lips before saying, "Let's go find that motorbike."

PIPPA and I drive up to Ubud, the bustling yoga city in the heart of Bali's jungle. After checking into a massive villa and showering off the travel dust—I take her in the shower, the two of us coming together under the spray and finally able to scream so loud we're practically hoarse—Pippa demands we change into swimsuits and head to a tourist trap she's been dying to visit.

I'm still so floored by the stellar orgasm I'd agree to anything, so before I can convince her we should stay chained to the bed, I find myself back on the bike, Pippa pressed snugly against me as I weave around vehicles on our way to Tegenungan waterfall.

"Wow," says Pippa as we stare down from atop the cliff at the waterfall below. "It's even more beautiful in person."

Even I have to admit that's the case, although usually I loathe tourist traps with a fiery passion. This one is no different; people are everywhere, walking down the steep steps to the waterfall, browsing in the outdoor stalls lining the way to those steps, lounging in the only bar at the top of said steps. Just the thought of being around all these people makes me want to head back the way we came, but one look at Pippa's excited face has me resigning myself to the inevitable.

Pippa takes my hand, which somehow makes the crowd worth it, and begins weaving through everyone, her small pack banging on her back. We make our way down the winding stairs to the bottom, then step over the rocks to the other side of the stream that barrels away from the waterfall. Down here it's fortunately less crowded, and when we finally reach the base of the waterfall, I reluctantly admit the crowds may have been worth it.

"Wow," I say, staring up at the watery cascade. "That's not bad, huh?"

I glance over; Pippa is pulling off her shirt to reveal her red bikini top. My mouth instantly runs dry, my dick twitching.

"What are you doing?" I croak.

She nods toward the water. "What, are you telling me you're not going to swim under the stupidly gorgeous waterfall?"

"The only thing here that's stupidly gorgeous is you," I huff, peeling off my own shirt. "The waterfall is just pretty."

She blushes. "Thank you, Schiller. Keep those kinds of compliments coming and you might earn a reward later."

My head whips toward her, my shirt forgotten. "Oh really?"

She nods, then slowly slides her shorts provocatively over her hips, down her endless legs to her ankles, where she kicks them off. I groan, instantly hard; I step into the water before I can completely embarrass myself. Pippa smirks, like she knows exactly what she's just done to me, then shoves her clothes into her pack, along with my shirt when I throw it to her, and then tosses it on the rocks at her feet.

"Aren't you worried someone might take that?" I ask.

She shrugs, swimming closer until we're inches apart. "It's just a towel and some clothes. We locked our phones in the bike and my wrist wallet is waterproof." She holds up her wrist, debit cards and ID shimmering up at me through the waterproof plastic. "There's nothing in my pack of value. If something happens to it, the swim here, with you, under the waterfall, will be worth the loss."

I stare at her, the words hitting me harder than expected. What must that be like, to have so little attachment to your own possessions? Virtually everything I had growing up was either inherited or would one day be inherited or was simply too expensive to risk breaking it, let alone just letting someone steal it. Even now, years after essentially walking away from my family's company and my inheritance—apart from splurging occasionally on things like our villa—the idea of being so cavalier about my possessions seems wrong.

Shouldn't it be the other way around? She's told me how dire her financial situation is. Shouldn't she be concerned about protecting whatever she has left? And if she's not, is that because she's truly one of those people who's not defined by material goods?

Or is her situation not as dire as she's led me to believe?

Pippa doesn't give me the chance to ask, because she takes off toward the waterfall, her body moving sensually through the water, as entrancing now as she is at sixty feet deep.

I follow, catching her just as she reaches the water and dives under, swimming down to the bottom. Taking a deep breath, I dive below as well, kicking furiously under the falls. The water pummels my back as I swim; once it falls away, I make for the surface, popping up behind Pippa.

We're in a little alcove, blocked from view, the faint chatter of people barely discernible over the roar of the falls. Pippa laughs and floats on her back. I join her and she takes my hand. We drift like we did with the Mola mola, the water cascading over us.

"You know," she says after we float lazily for a few minutes. "I was planning to just swim for a bit, but then I noticed your situation."

"What situation?"

She glances over at me, lips curving in a smile that's decidedly naughty as she says, "Your erect dick, obviously. You really like my bikini, don't you?"

"Pippa," I growl in warning. "We're in a public place."

She throws her free hand wide. "I don't see anyone, do you?"

"That's ... we can't ... don't even think about it."

Pippa stops floating, straightening and jerking me toward her. She throws a glance over my shoulder to verify no one is around, drags me flush against her, and throws her arms around my neck.

"Schiller," she growls in my ear, "by now, I've sucked

you enough times to know how to make you come inside a minute. Stand up."

"Fuck," I say, getting to my feet without stopping to think of how easily someone might spot us. The water is surprisingly shallow this close to the rock wall; Pippa has no troubling kneeling before me, her nimble fingers drawing me out of my suit. She moans softly at the sight of me and then lowers her head to wrap her wet mouth around my aching cock.

"Jesus," I groan, burying my hand in her hair and guiding her deeper down my length.

Pippa moans around me. I jerk, my fist dragging her head back before I can plunge too deep. She makes a sound of protest and grips the base of my cock, squeezing hard as she pumps in time with her mouth.

"Shit, you're going to make me come too fast," I cry.

"Hey, I think someone is in there!" someone calls through the water. "What's it like in there? Can you swim in under the falls?"

"Fuck, they're going to find us," I pant down at her, watching her head bob faster and faster up and down my shaft. She cups my balls, massaging them softly as she fully withdraws and licks the head of my cock. "Pip, we better ... you better ... stop."

Her eyes flick up at me, lips curving as she takes me inside her again. My fist tightens in her hair, feeling the crest of my orgasm begin to take me. I groan, throwing my head back, intent on pulling her off me, but her arms come around me, holding my cock deep inside her mouth. I explode, hips bucking against her once, twice, before falling still. I gape down at her, chest heaving.

"You're going to pay for that later."

Pippa merely winks at me, tucking my cock back inside my suit and jerking it up over my hips just as a group swims up into our hidden oasis.

CHAPTER TWELVE

PIPPA

S chiller and I swim off as the group frolics behind the waterfall. He's staring at me again, a coiled intensity about him. I bite back a smug smile; he's always going on about not getting caught, but whenever I seduce him anyway, he goes off like a rocket.

He enjoys the naughtiness of it just as much as I do.

Unfortunately, there's no place for him to make me pay. There are people everywhere, and I'm not into outright exhibitionism. So instead, we gather my bag from its spot on the rocks—no one thought to even go through it—and towel off.

Schiller holds the towel out of my reach. I make a swipe for it, but he just grins wickedly and begins toweling me off himself. By the time he reaches my shoulders, I'm practically ready to give exhibitionism a try. But he just winks and swipes quickly at his own body before stuffing the towel back in my bag. We pull our clothes on and start the hike back up to the top of the ravine.

He takes my hand as we walk and squeezes it; I smile up at him and swing our hands between us. He laughs in surprise, pulling me closer. And I'm not exactly sure how I know, but I'm entirely convinced that he's never found himself in a relationship that's physically affectionate. Now that we're in ... whatever this is between us, he finds that he enjoys the simple pleasure of holding someone's hand.

The realization saddens me; what must his childhood have been like, if holding hands is something that surprises him? That must have been awful in combination with all those crappy women who dated him only for his money. He hasn't exactly spelled that out, but it seems only logical that's what happened. For however long this lasts, I'm going to show him that there's another way to be, and even if we go our separate ways, he'll know there are some women who value simple physical affection and emotional intimacy.

We finally make it back to the top of the ravine. My eyes land on the vendors and excitement courses through me. Now here's another thing I'd like to do!

Before I left the boat for the weekend, Lachlan paid me the wages I've incurred so far. I haven't been this flush with cash in ages, and it's wonderful to feel the boot of poverty lift from my neck, at least for a little while. I feel like celebrating. And right now, with nothing planned for the rest of the day, I intend to do a little harmless shopping.

The only thing, though, is that when he passed me the wad of bills, Lachlan gave me the impression that he hadn't paid the rest of the crew their part, probably to ensure they come back after the weekend, which didn't sit well with me.

When I tried to ask about it, he brushed me off and changed the subject. Definitely shady. This job means a lot to Made and the rest of the crew, so the whole situation pisses me off, because now I feel like I have to hide the fact that I got paid myself so no one else feels bad—or even worse, outright scammed.

I'm glad Schiller and I decided to come up to Ubud, because it's unlikely we'll run into anyone else from the ship, and thus I won't have to outright lie. Same goes for Schiller; as long as he doesn't ask, I'm not going to tell him, because I know Made has become his friend, and I don't want Schiller to worry that Lachlan might be thinking of skipping out on paying his crew. Not when I don't have any proof of that yet.

I hate Lachlan for putting me in this situation. The thought hadn't even occurred to me until today. Just what the hell is he planning, exactly?

But there's nothing I can do about any of that.

"Hey, Schill," I say.

"Hmm?" he says absently, staring at our intertwined hands.

I nod toward the booths. "If you're not in a rush, can I look at some of the stalls for a bit? I've wanted to check out the batik fabric since I arrived in Bali and haven't had the chance yet."

Schiller's gaze flicks from the vendors to me, confusion flashing in his eyes. I almost break down and tell him right there about my windfall. If he asks me outright, I'll surely tell him, but if he doesn't, I'd prefer to keep the whole thing to myself for now, especially my growing suspicions about Lachlan. I don't want to just accuse a person without being certain, and Schiller is on his boat to get closure for his godfather in the first place. If I share my suspicions with him, he might feel conflicted about continuing to work for the man. What if he quit because of something I haven't yet verified, and then Lachlan went on to find the boat? That would be horrible.

"Sure," he says slowly. "But I'm not much of a shopper, so I'll just hang out at that bar over there, if that's okay?"

"Yeah, that's fine," I say absently, already studying the booths. Wow, they really make beautiful fabric here, don't they? And those little wicker purses are so cute. I'm not really a purse woman, but I kind of want one of those. "I'll meet you over there once I'm finished. I'm sure I'll want a cold drink after walking around so much in this heat."

"Take your time."

Schiller extricates his hand from mine. I send him one last smile and then disappear into the market, feeling his eyes on my back. Humming to myself, I weave around the booths, walking from end-to-end to get a feel for the place before I settle on a place to peruse.

Like most tourist traps, the vendors are selling mostly the same things, but it's still pleasant to take a stroll through them, and there are a few small differences. I settle on one of the vendors at the end, situated so far away I can barely see the bar where Schiller's waiting.

Running my hands through the multi-colored fabric, I wonder what I should get. I have to purchase *something*—batik fabric is unbelievably gorgeous and practically a symbol of Indonesia—but it's understandably also expensive, since it's time-consuming and requires skill to make.

And while I just got paid five grand, I'd like to not immediately spend it all. I suspect the villa Schiller rented is insanely expensive. While there's no way I can afford to pay my half of it, I still want to pay something, otherwise it just feels like I'm mooching off him. If we were in an actual relationship, that might be one thing, but we're not.

So probably a small piece of batik. Maybe a scarf? A handkerchief? I never use those, but it's so hot here I'm sweating all the time, so maybe ... And then there's those little wicker purses that are so cute.

No, I'll just get the handkerchief; it's a good reminder of my time here, but it won't break the bank. I select one with pale pink and yellow stripes, and then on impulse, I pick one for Schiller as well, the fabric the same intense ocean-blue of his eyes. It has alternating blue-and-green diamonds that for some strange reason remind me of the Mola mola drifting through the water.

"Batik is always so beautiful, isn't it?"

"Hmm?" I say, still staring at my handkerchiefs, my thumb caressing the patterns.

"The batik. You made some beautiful choices there. A gift for someone?"

I lift my gaze. An older man is standing before me, his hair and neatly trimmed beard shock-white. The brightness of his hair is further underscored by the white suit he's wearing, made of linen. A navy ascot is tied jauntily around his neck and he holds a blue hat negligently at his side. A gold watch so obviously expensive it makes me fear for his general safety adorns one wrist.

What is this guy doing here? He seems like he'd fit in nicely in Seminyak, or at that Rock Bar near Uluwatu, but some random waterfall? Full of sweaty tourists and clutter? Not really.

But maybe he's just a sightseer like the rest of us.

"Oh, uh, yeah," I say. "Well, just the one is a gift. The other is for me."

The man smiles then says in a voice tinged with an American accent, "May I?"

"Sure," I say, passing them over. He runs his thumb over the fabric.

"I assume the pink is for you?"

I shrug. "Guilty."

He laughs softly. "I don't blame you. I find I'm rather partial to that pink myself. Although I suspect the blue one would go better with my outfit."

He holds it up to his breast pocket, as if modeling the potential addition. An irrational fear sweeps through me that he might decide to take it for himself, which is ridiculous. I haven't even bought the thing yet and am uncertain that Schiller would even like it.

The man hands them back. "I think he'll like it."

"How do you know it's for a man?"

He nods toward the bar. "I was down at the waterfall

earlier. What a trip with these old knees! Barely made it. But I believe I saw you with a man, yes? Tall, black hair?"

"Oh. Yeah ..." I say, suddenly suspicious. Did he just happen to notice us walking, or is he *watching*? I'm a nobody, but Schiller isn't, now that I think about it. He doesn't talk about it, but wouldn't being an heir to that much wealth make you a target? Is this guy scoping us out for something? Maybe I should head back to Schiller.

The man throws his hand up as if guessing my thoughts. "Oh, don't worry, dear. I just noticed because I could have sworn I saw the two of you getting off a yacht in Sanur this morning. My own vessel—much more humble, I have to admit—was docked a few slips down, and I just thought it would be so coincidental that we would then run into each other here."

"Small world," I say, suspicion only slightly assuaged. The man *does* look as if he'd own a yacht at that port, so probably that part of his story lines up. "Well, I'll probably head—"

"Do you think you could probably help me pick out something for my nephew? Shopping matters tend to go over my head."

"Sure," I say, not wanting to but also seeing no overt reason to be outright rude to the guy. "How old is he?"

"I imagine he's around your age."

"Well," I say, scanning the booth. "Maybe a shirt? Unless you want to get him a handkerchief like I did, most of this stuff here I feel like women are going to enjoy more."

The man frowns, shoulders slumping with such

genuine disappointment I begin to believe his story. "I suppose you're right. I should probably just get him a gadget or something. Who wants random souvenirs anymore?"

Yikes. The last thing I need on my conscience is accidentally making the guy feel bad. "There are also those leather wristbands there. Maybe one of those? They're a little more discreet in case he's not a bright shirt kind of person."

"That's also a nice option," the man says distractedly. He suddenly turns to me. "Correct me if I'm wrong, but the boat you disembarked from; that vessel belongs to Miles Lachlan, yes?"

I blink at him.

He waves his hand again. "It's a well-known boat on this island, I'm afraid."

"I see," I say, knowing it's probably the truth but still not quite believing him. "My ... friend and I have been part of a dive crew for him for a few days now."

His expression sharpens with interest. "I see. Looking for anything interesting?"

"How would you know that?"

He shrugs. "Someone is always looking for something in Bali. Lachlan is no different."

"How do you know him?" I ask.

"Oh, everyone knows him. He's been around here a long time."

I frown. "It was my understanding that Lachlan is new to the island."

"No, Miss. He most certainly is not," the man says. He sends a troubled look toward the bar, then returns his attention to me. "Now, I know I'm just a stranger to you, but you seem like a nice woman, you helped me with my nephew, and I feel a sense of obligation. Take it from an old man who's been around a while: you would do well—the two of you—if you broke off any association you have with Miles Lachlan. He's treated most of the people working at the port atrociously, and this is just his latest venture. Whatever he has planned, you don't want to be involved in it. Find another person to dive for; there are surely many searching for divers like yourselves."

"I see," I say slowly.

The man smiles at me. "Well, thank you for the shopping tips. I believe I'll get one of those wristbands like you suggested. Enjoy the rest of your weekend."

He selects one of the wristbands, then strolls over to the seller, who smiles at him and wraps it carefully when the man requests her to do so. He places the package in his breast pocket, smiles a final time at me, then walks to an idling town car, whose driver comes out to open the back door for him. The man settles inside, and the driver returns behind the wheel. Within seconds, the car has disappeared onto the busy road.

How many people are going to keep warning me away from Lachlan?

And how many more will I need to hear before I heed their advice?

CHAPTER THIRTEEN

SCHILLER

Made calls me the following morning.

"Yeah?" I say quietly, not wanting to wake Pippa who's still sleeping naked in bed. Padding out onto the veranda, I quietly shut the sliding door and then say, "What do you need?"

"Just verifying you'll be back at the boat tomorrow morning."

"Of course I will," I say in confusion. "Why wouldn't I be?"

Made pauses before replying, "I just thought ... with Pippa ... you might be interested in other things."

"That's not the case at all," I say, staring through the window at her. She suddenly rolls over on her back, exposing a breast. Need slams through me as my cock hardens. I turn my back on the sight, hoping to get Made off the phone quickly so I can get back to her. "Why would you think that?"

"Because you disappeared with her for the weekend," he says dryly.

"Well, though that is the case, I will be returning for the second half of the trip. We both will be."

"Perhaps you should consider chartering your own vessel to find the wreck. Why do you need Lachlan to do that?"

"I don't need him at all," I say. "I joined to prevent him from finding it. I don't want anyone but me finding the *Galvanizer*, and so far, I've yet to do so. So whenever someone gets it in their head to go find it, I either try to dissuade them of that notion or, failing that, work my way on board and gently steer them in the wrong direction."

"Why are you doing that? I assume it has something to do with your personal relation to Galvan?"

"I won't allow my godfather's death to be made a spectacle of," I say. "No one else will care about him if it's found; they'll just want whatever else they find on that ship. And there will inevitably be a fight between Galvan's estate and whoever finds it. I won't let that happen. I'm going to be the one to find it—or no one will at all. If that means yanking Lachlan's chain for a few weeks, then so—"

"Look," Made suddenly says, "I called to say that Pippa —and you, no, all of us—shouldn't return to Lachlan. Period. And you certainly shouldn't risk angering him by deliberately leading him away from the wreck."

"What?" I bark. "Why do you keep pushing this?"

Made sighs. "His associate showed up, okay? And I know the man. Or rather, my father knows him. He used to work for an outfit that the man, Alastair, ran about a decade ago. My father wasn't aware of it when he was hired, but he later learned that Alastair was running guns between Java and Bali for some of the fundamentalist groups. In horribly large quantities, too.

"My father quit immediately once he discovered it, but it wasn't the most graceful exit. They weren't pleased but couldn't determine how much he learned about their outfit, so they had to let him go. Alastair never met me, but I can't be certain whether he might recognize me because of my father.

"What do you think might happen if we're on that boat, multiple days out from the island, and he suddenly puts it together? Do you want to take that risk? I don't. He might link me back to my father. He might link you to Galvan, too, which could put you in danger as well. For whatever reason, Lachlan is dead set on finding that wreck. Alastair must be involved. It's just not worth it. I know you want to find your godfather's grave, but—"

"Wait, how did you find out I knew Galvan in the first place?" I say, suddenly realizing I never told Made that.

"Bentley hinted," he says quickly. "It is not my intention to overstep the bounds of our relationship. I just don't want something to happen to you. But if I declined to return tomorrow, I would wonder about your safety."

I sigh. "I know your intentions are good, Made. I'm not upset, and I'm obviously glad you brought this to my attention. I had no idea Lachlan was such a criminal. Does he work for Alastair? Is he a partner?"

"I'm not sure," says Made slowly. "Something tells me Lachlan works for him."

"You don't think they're running guns aboard with us, do you?"

Made doesn't reply.

I swear. "Unbelievable."

"It really is concerning. That's why I think it would be better if we didn't return."

"Oh, I'm seeing this through," I say.

"What?" Made says in alarm. "Why?"

"It's my godfather," I say. "What if Lachlan actually found his wreck? I'll be damned if I let that man be the one to find him. Why does he even want to find it so badly in the first place? An arms dealer, looking for treasure?"

"Perhaps it's a front to run guns," Made muses. "We're always asleep at night, and we're far enough out that we're in international waters. Maybe they move them at night. We've certainly provided them with adequate cover for being there."

"Christ," I say, plowing a hand through my hair. "So you think it's a front, then? Hell, we could be accessories!"

"I don't think that would happen," says Made quietly. "First, the authorities would have to intercept us, and secondly, you're well-documented as being a diver. Not to mention you're related to the man who owned the ship that wrecked. You're known throughout the world for trying to find it. There'd be no other reason for you to be on board. And I haven't found any evidence of them even running guns at all."

"So he really is trying to find the wreck, then."

"Probably."

"Fuck, what a nightmare," I sigh.

Made stays silent a long time, then says, "So you are determined to see it through to the end, then?"

I sigh again. "I've come this far; I'm not going to let him get away with whatever it is he's trying to do. If it turns out he really is running guns, I'm going to report it when we return to Bali."

Made makes a distressed noise. "For the record, I don't agree with this."

"I'm certainly not asking you to come with me."

"But I will. I'm not leaving you alone on that boat."

"I'm sure it will be fine."

"Tate ... what about Pippa?"

I glance over my shoulder. "What about her?"

"Tate. She can't possibly return to that boat."

"What are you asking, that I should demand she stay away? Bar her from boarding again?"

"That's exactly what I'm saying."

"I will certainly tell her what you just told me, but I can't keep her from doing what she wants. I'm not ... we don't ... our relationship isn't like that."

"Hmm."

"And she really needs the money," I add, although a small part of me wonders whether that's true. She's been a little off since the waterfall, where she bought a bunch of trinkets. Then last night at dinner she insisted on paying, and it wasn't exactly inexpensive. Where is she getting all this money from? Wasn't she robbed?

Is there some other reason she wants to be on that boat? She couldn't—no, I refuse to believe she's involved in whatever Lachlan is doing. I just can't believe that.

But still, something doesn't add up, and she hasn't been quite as carefree since the waterfall.

"Tate," Made says sharply, interrupting my thoughts, "if you care about that woman at all—at *all*, Tate—you'll do whatever necessary to keep her off that boat!"

"Jesus, Made," I say, shocked by his outburst. He's never raised his voice before in the short time I've known him. "I get it, okay? I'll make sure she knows the score."

"Good," he says, "then if you insist on proceeding—and I hope you won't—I'll see you on the dock tomorrow morning."

"See you then," I say, hanging up.

Heading back inside, I toss my phone on the bedside table and stare at Pippa. She's stretched out along the brilliantly white sheets, her pale blonde hair virtually fading into them. Her entire left side has escaped the sheet from shoulder to toe, revealing a long line of soft skin I ache to taste.

She moans, head rolling on the pillow. Slowly, her eyes open and scan the room before landing on me.

"Hey," she says sleepily, her voice husky from all the screams I drew out of her last night. "Did you sleep well?"

I grin and prowl toward her, crawling up from the foot of the bed, my mouth nibbling lightly up the length of her body. When I reach her mouth, I take it quickly in a deep kiss before whispering against it, "Did you? I barely let you get any sleep."

She squirms beneath me. "More like the other way around. I seem to recall *you* begging to stop that last time."

"Well, now, we can't have that," I say, pulling back the covers and rolling onto her. Bending down, I draw a tight nipple into my mouth; she hums with pleasure and lazily drags her hands through my hair, her nails sending tingles down my spine.

Pippa spreads her legs wide, allowing me to nestle between them as I kiss up the column of her throat until I reach her mouth. We fall into a kiss, tongues leisurely tangling until minutes later she suddenly pulls away.

"I wasn't finished with your mouth," I grumble, head dipping toward her again, but she laughs and throws up a finger to stop me.

"I have something for you," she says.

"Really?"

She nods, then reaches for her purse on the table next to us. Her hand roots around inside before pulling out a small square of fabric.

My throat tightens. Is this what she was buying yesterday, when I wondered how she was spending all this money? She bought something for *me*?

No one buys anything for me. Not without strings attached.

"It's not much," she says, almost shyly. "But I don't

know. It seemed like a nice memory. I got one too, but this one reminded me of your eyes."

"It's beautiful," I murmur as she hands it to me. She's right; it has a similar color to my eyes. "Which one did you get?"

She reaches back into her bag and retrieves the other one, holding it out to me. I run my thumbs over both of them, something about seeing the two pieces mixed together making it suddenly hard to breathe.

"I want yours," I say.

"You want a pink-and-yellow one?" she asks in surprise.

"I want the one that will remind me of you—not me," I say tightly. I kiss her again, before adding, "As I'd hope you would want the one that reminds you of me."

She blinks rapidly, the emotion in her eyes making my own burn. "I like that," she says softly, and hands me the pink one.

Taking the blue one as well, I place them on the table where we can both see them, and then enter her in one long thrust. Pippa throws her arms around my neck and moves with me, both of us whispering soft words to the other as I ride us both to ecstasy.

I don't think about what Made told me. I don't think about the fact that I'm going to have to tell Pippa she can't return, which will prevent her from earning the money she needs.

And I especially ignore the reality that I'll also have to tell her that I will be staying on, therefore ending what we have right here in this bed. This was always supposed to be temporary; people don't meet the love of their life on some boat, and I won't delude myself thinking this is the exception.

So our time is limited. This too shall end. But I'm not going to tell her yet. Let there be one more day. One last, perfect day before it all ends.

CHAPTER FOURTEEN

PIPPA

Schiller proclaims that we're going somewhere special for dinner. He doesn't say what "special" entails, but I'm almost certain it means "expensive." I choose not to fret about how I'll contribute my portion, and instead put on the dress I have with me, which isn't that nice but still makes Schiller's face grow dark with desire.

"I've never seen you in a dress before," he growls in appreciation, eyes locked on my legs, bare from the mid-thigh down.

"This is true," I say, tossing the hem of the black dress jauntily.

He swallows hard. "Or heels, for that matter."

"They're the only ones I own."

His head jerks up. "Really?"

"Only dress, too. I spend most of my life in a swimsuit. Don't exactly need a bunch of dresses."

Schiller blinks slowly, then snakes an arm around my

waist. "The swimsuits that also keep me perpetually half-hard."

He buries his head in my neck as I say, "An added bonus."

Schiller's arm tightens around me. I can feel him growing stiff against my stomach. In a few moments, I'm going to be tossed on this bed, and then we'll never make the meal. While I certainly wouldn't complain, Schiller's been going on enough about this dinner that I don't want us to miss it.

"Our reservation is soon," I say against his ear.

"Hmm, you're right." He pulls away with obvious reluctance, taking my hand in his and leading us from the villa.

Instead of leading me to the motorbike, he turns toward a black town car parked at the end of the drive. I raise my brows at him.

"Did you think I'd expect you to head over on the back of a bike in that dress?"

I snort. "I suppose not."

He opens the door, letting me slide inside and then getting in after me. He throws an arm over my shoulder as the car pulls away.

"So are you going to tell me where we're going now?"

Schiller drops a kiss onto my forehead. "No, I think I'll keep it a surprise."

"You know, Schill," I say, growing serious, "I'm looking forward to this evening but I'm afraid it's going to be a bit outside my price range."

He squeezes my shoulder, tucking me under his chin. "Don't worry about it."

"It doesn't seem right for me to—"

"I want to do it, Pippa," he whispers to me, and there's a strange hitch in his voice, like he struggles to get the words out. Something's missing here, but I also get the sense that he wants tonight to be pleasant, so I let it drop.

"Thank you," I say instead. He kisses my forehead again and we fall into contented silence, watching the Balinese scenery speed past on the way to our destination.

We pull into a hotel along the southern coast an hour later. I raise my brows at him. A hotel restaurant? He just smiles and shakes his head.

"You're really going to keep this a secret until the end, aren't you?"

He grins. "It's more fun that way."

We exit the car, walk through the hotel and then out into incredible gardens that wind along a path to the edge of the cliff the hotel is perched atop.

"Um, I hate to be the bearer of bad news," I say, "but we appear to be running out of land."

"Are we?"

Schiller halts in front of a door that's hewn straight into the rock, which opens to reveal an elevator. We take it down; a few seconds later it opens onto a bar cut right into the middle of the cliff. The walls are made of glass, allowing us to stare straight down into the water below. Out across the horizon, the setting sun bathes everything in brilliant red.

"Oh, my God! It's the Rock Bar," I breathe, staring in astonishment at the ocean crashing against the cliff many feet below. "This is stunning. I've seen photos before, but they pale in comparison to the real thing."

"I thought you would like it," he says, nodding to one of the hostesses before giving her his name. We're seated at an intimate table in the corner, away from the rest of the tables and affording a perfect view of the sun setting over the Indian Ocean.

Schiller pulls out the chair facing the water, waits for me to situate myself and then pushes it in behind me. He takes the chair opposite.

"Here, move your chair around so that we can both see the ocean," I say, reaching for the arm of his chair. A view like this should be shared.

His hand covers mine. "I don't want to see the ocean. I want to see you."

My eyes fly to his. He grins slowly at me, his smile growing wider when he notices my blush. "You say such casually erotic things, Schiller."

The grin turns wicked. He leans forward, hand squeezing mine as he murmurs, "That's because I love making your eyes light up with desire. Just as they are right now. They look just like that when I make you come."

"*Schiller*," I say shakily, glancing at the other tables around us. "People are going to overhear you."

"They're far too busy with themselves to pay me any attention."

"Still," I say, deciding I'd better take a moment to come

to terms with the magnitude of what Schiller's done for me before I do something inadvisable, like have my way with him right here on this table. "I'm going to head to the restroom for a moment."

He gives me a long look that has need pulsing through me. "Shall I join you?"

"Of course not!"

He winks. "If you change your mind, you know where to find me."

I roll my eyes and get up from the table, knees weak. Schiller's entire face lights up when he realizes the effect he's had on me. It makes him look younger, boyish almost, and terribly sexy. I run a hand absently over the crown of his head as I head for the bathroom. He growls at me and bites the inside of my wrist, then lets me go. His gaze drills into my back as I weave around the other tables, feeling dizzy.

He said he wanted to do something special, but I would never have assumed he meant something like *this*. It's undoubtedly one of the most beautiful places I've ever seen in my life; I want to make a bed under our table and never leave.

In the bathroom, I give myself a quick pep talk to remind myself it would be a terrible idea to lose my head over Schiller Tate. While we've certainly been having fun together, nothing about this strikes me as a permanent relationship. The last thing I want is to fall for him and be forced to deal with that once we go our separate ways.

After giving myself a firm talking-to, I return to our

table and we have an absolutely amazing meal. And while the food is positively drool worthy, more than anything else I enjoy the company. Until now we've never gone on a real date, and it catches both of us by surprise how easy it is between us.

By the time our desserts arrive, I'm full and happy and so aroused I can hardly stand it. If the expression in Schiller's eyes is anything to go by, I'm not the only one.

Glancing around for the first time in what feels like hours, I do a double take. Is that? It *is*. The guy from the waterfall! What the hell is he doing here? I watch as he's served a drink at the bar; he takes a small sip, his back to us, then glances over his shoulder casually.

Our eyes collide. Mine narrow. He blinks, as if surprised, then raises his glass in salute.

Yeah, no. This is too weird. Way too coincidental. I glance at Schiller; he's cutting into his desert without a care in the world.

"I'll be right back," I say, then get up before he has a chance to reply.

The man smiles at me once I stop in front of him. "What a crazy coincidence," I say.

He shrugs. "This is the best restaurant on the island, no? It isn't a complete stretch."

"Hmm," I say. "Perhaps we should introduce ourselves. I'm Pippa."

"Pippa?"

"Turner."

"A pleasure," he says. "Can I buy you a drink, Ms. Turner?"

"Thank you, but no. I'm here with someone else."

"Right. The dark-haired man." He glances over my shoulder. Schiller is still eating his dessert but has semi-turned to view the ocean as he eats. As we watch, he takes the last bite and then pushes the plate away, a soft smile on his face as he stares out at the ocean.

"Yeah, that's my ... friend," I say, for lack of a better word.

"And he is Schiller Tate, yes?"

My eyes narrow. "Why would you think that?"

The man shrugs. "Oh, well, I'll confess that after I met you, I had the strangest feeling as if I'd seen your friend before. Once I arrived back at my yacht, I'm afraid I succumbed to the temptation of an internet search. Your man's name came up quite quickly." He becomes troubled. "I suppose Lachlan wanted to make a big to-do about what he was doing. There were multiple articles that he'd hired the man."

"You mean to go after the wreck?" I say slowly.

"Yes," he says absently. "The *Galvanizer*. So many people have tried to find that blasted boat. And now, here we are, with Mr. Tate trying to find it with Lachlan, of all people."

"I don't believe I've gotten your name yet," I say, ready to see if he will reveal such information about himself when I ask him point blank.

"Oh!" he says, taking another sip and then shaking his head, "Silly me. Call me Andrew. Andrew Lawrence."

"Right."

"But, Ms. Turner, now that our paths have happened to cross again, I do feel as though I have a duty to warn you off again from your endeavor."

"Is there anything left to say? I remember what you told me yesterday."

Andrew turns to look at me, his glass raised halfway to his mouth. "So you remember what I told you about avoiding any further association with Lachlan?"

"Yes, I recall," I say. "And I appreciate your concern. We're not due back to the boat until tomorrow morning."

"So there's still time."

"Excuse me?"

He shrugs. "Time to convince you to forgo continuing with this trip. You mustn't return."

"Look," I say, "like I said, I appreciate your desire to warn us. However, I don't know you. I'm sure you're well-meaning, but Schiller has personal reasons for wanting to find that boat himself. And I'm going to support him in that endeavor."

Andrew nods. "Yes, I can certainly understand why Tate, of all people, would want to find it. That doesn't mean you need to be around when that happens. Can't you convince him to give it up? There are forces at play here that I'm almost entirely certain that you're unaware of."

"What are you talking about?" I say, glancing at Schiller, my gut tightening with unease.

"So you don't know," Andrew says, shaking his head. "Perhaps not. I've been in this area for so many years, sometimes I forget that people don't know the full story of the *Galvanizer*."

"The ship went down with a bunch of wealth on board, and no one knows precisely where or when. Or even why, for that matter. But everyone wants to find it. Pretty cut and dry. What more is there for me to know?"

Andrew laughs, then, seeing my seriousness, falls silent, his expression transforming into one of concern. "There's more to it than that, Ms. Turner. Tate is Galvan's heir. If that ship is found, he inherits everything."

CHAPTER FIFTEEN

SCHILLER

Both of us feel dread when we wake Monday morning. For a moment, we lay in bed, neither moving, just staring at the ceiling.

Pippa rolls over on her stomach, the sheet slipping down her naked back. "Shall we get breakfast? That fruit from yesterday should still be good."

I absently stroke a palm down her back, mesmerized by the softness of her skin and the way the long strands of her hair fall over her body.

I've put it off as long as I can. There's no more time, so few minutes remaining. I wanted last night to be special, a memory for each of us to keep once we part ways.

"We could," I say quietly, "or I could make love to you one last time."

She stills, gaze locked on mine. "One last time?"

She doesn't comment on the other part of the statement; both of us know that when we returned last night, the way we reached for each other had obviously changed from fucking to lovemaking.

I sigh, pulling my hand away. "You can't return to the ship, Pippa."

"Why not?"

"Made called yesterday morning. You were still asleep."

Her face tightens with concern. "What did he call about?"

"He told me about Lachlan's associate. Apparently, they both run guns between some of the islands in Indonesia."

"*What?*"

"Yeah," I sigh again. "And have apparently been doing it for a while now."

"Oh my God," she says, looking horrified. She pales. "You don't ... Lachlan hasn't been doing it onboard while *we* were there, right?"

My silence is answer enough.

Pippa jerks upright. "I can't believe that! I mean, I'd been warned that Lachlan was a bad guy, but—"

"Who told you that?" I ask.

"Made—and his dad, actually. When I first got hired. I just thought he was an asshole, but apparently, it's way worse than that. Neither of them really wanted me to sign onto that ship. I just ... didn't have any other options."

"I know," I say quietly. "If you're worried about the wages you will lose, I'll write you a check myself, but you can't go back on that boat. There's no evidence that they're actually running guns right under our noses, but us being there would definitely provide useful cover."

"Oh God, what if they saw us!"

"What are you talking about?"

She flushes. "That first night. On deck. When we ..."

Fury snaps through me. Fuck, I hadn't even considered that. That someone might have witnessed one of the most erotic moments of my life makes me want to hunt down the bastards hiding on the ship and deal with them myself.

"I'm sure no one saw us," I say instead, hating that the thought has occurred to her. "We were talking for a while before, and no one was around. We would have heard or seen them. If they did make a deal, it must have been on a different date. Or maybe it will be happening now that the associate—his name is Alastair—has arrived. Don't think like that, okay?"

She sighs, then straightens. "Oh, and don't worry about the money. Lachlan gave me the wages I'd incurred up until that point. I'm all paid up."

I roll toward her. "Are you serious?"

She laughs. "Well, how else did you think I paid for the meals and your batik handkerchief? I didn't say anything, but I assumed you must have figured it out, anyway."

My chest tightens at the realization that one of the first things she did after getting paid money she desperately needed was spend it on me. And here I've been wondering if she was misrepresenting the seriousness of her financial situation.

"You shouldn't have spent that on me," I say past a lump in my throat.

"I was happy to do it."

She was happy to do it. Just like I'd been happy to pay for this villa, and the dinner last night, and the car, and everything else. But me paying for her and the other way around aren't nearly the same thing; I've got more money than I could spend in this lifetime. Paying for these things won't make any noticeable difference for me.

For her, though, it will.

"Why didn't you tell me he paid you?" I ask, now wondering if she'd meant to keep it from me.

She shrugs. "Lachlan hasn't paid the others and Made said that the job means a lot to the locals. I didn't want anyone to feel bad that I had gotten paid before them."

My eyes narrow, part of my discussion with Made returning to me. "Why'd he pay you and no one else?"

"To be honest? No idea. I've been wondering that myself. I asked him and he refused to answer."

"You weren't expecting to cut out early, then?"

She blinks at me. "Of course not. I'd like the additional money I'd earn from the remainder of the trip, and I also know how important it is to you to find the wreck. I wanted to be there for you if that happened."

Ignoring the warmth her words elicit, I say, "He's not going to find the wreck."

"How do you know that?"

"How do you not? I already told you I'm going to lead him away from it."

Pippa gapes at me. "What? You're going back?"

I lean up myself. "Of course."

"Of course? *Of course*? You can't seriously be planning to go back there after what Made told you?"

My jaws clench. "Yes."

"Schiller, no!"

I cast my eyes away from her.

"But it could be so dangerous! What's going to happen if you see them making a deal and they catch you? They'd protect themselves. You might be killed!"

"They're not going to kill me," I scoff, anger rolling through me. Does she think I *like* any of this? Does she think I'm excited about potentially walking into the belly of the beast? She must know I've already considered all of this and still decided to do it anyway.

Pippa continues, "They certainly could kill you if they thought it necessary. You don't know that. They're a bunch of criminals, for God's sake."

"I won't be alone," I say. "Bentley and Made will be there. They aren't going to dump a trio of bodies and come back without us. It would be too damn suspicious, both to the authorities and the rest of the team."

"Just don't go!" she cries. "Don't do it, Schiller. It isn't worth it."

"It is to me!" I snap, unable to keep the tight leash on my emotions any longer. I wish this weren't happening, but it is. I finish what I start, and this, the most important thing of all, the thing that gave my previously vapid life purpose, won't be the one thing I quit.

"I'm not saying stop looking for your godfather's grave," she pleads. "I'm asking you to stop doing it with Lachlan."

"I have to *stop* Lachlan! What happens if a gunrunner finds a hundred million dollars in sunken treasure? Where is that all going to go? Not into the legitimate economy, let me tell you. Can you imagine how much terror a hundred million dollars might finance? Not to mention all that art lost to the black market!"

"Is that really what this is about?" she says. "Are you trying to find his grave or trying to find what you'll stand to inherit?"

My head snaps back. I roll out of bed, grabbing my suit pants from where I kicked them to the floor last night and yank them up over my legs, my movements jerky. Finally I turn to her. She's sitting up in bed, sheet clutched to her chest. I will myself not to become distracted by the sight of her.

"Where did you hear that?"

She sags. "So it is true."

"Was it Bentley?" Did my friend do this? Did he share my personal information with her? And if so, who should I be more pissed off at—him for the betrayal, or her for throwing it in my face right now?

"No, it wasn't Bentley," she snaps.

"Then who was it!"

She stares at me. "It was just an old man. An American who's been living here for years. Apparently he's been here since it happened and recognized you. It was a stranger."

"But how would he *know*? I don't tell anyone! It's not public knowledge!"

"Why hide it, Tate?"

"Oh, so I'm back to being Tate, now, am I?"

"When I suddenly discover you might have been lying to me this entire time, yeah, I put some emotional distance between us!"

I plow a hand through my hair. "I never lied to you."

"No, you just didn't tell the truth."

"For fuck's sake, Pippa, think about it!" I snap. "Do you think anyone would hire me to look for that wreck if they knew I'd stand to inherit it all if we found it? Galvan kept the details of his will private; I only found out about being his heir decades after he died!"

She climbs out of bed, bringing the sheet with her. "And they would kind of have a point in protesting, wouldn't they?"

"Why does it even matter so much? You already know I've distanced myself from my wealth. I don't think you understand how much I stand to inherit, Pippa. What's a little more I don't care about?"

She laughs bitterly. "A little more? Are you serious? You may have *distanced* yourself from your money, Tate, but only an absurdly wealthy person could ever call a hundred million dollars 'a little more.'

"And the problem I had with this is not that you'll inherit it at all, but that you didn't disclose it to me in the first place. I told you my parents want me to marry someone who's obsessed with making money! You *knew* I literally fled across the world to escape that.

"I thought you were different than those men. I thought you'd removed yourself from that kind of life. And now, because you lied, I just don't know which version to believe. The one you told me about that night on deck? Or the one I'm learning about now? Why didn't you just tell me?"

"Well, why should I have had to tell you such personal information to begin with when this isn't a real relationship, anyway?"

Silence falls at that. Pippa stares down at the floor for a long time. Shame and regret twist in my gut. I didn't mean to put it that harshly. And I wish ... things might have been different, once. But too late. At least now she'll be safer since she won't be near me anymore.

Pippa begins slowly picking her clothes off the floor, her back to me. "No, Tate, I suppose we're not."

"Pippa—"

"No, no. It's fine. You're right. This was just a little fun, right? And we've clearly had our differences from the start. No real relationship, as you put it, could ever have that kind of foundation and last for long."

"This has gotten out of hand," I say, hating how our discussion has devolved, hating that with one careless sentence, I just crushed the meaning out of everything we experienced these last weeks.

Pippa pulls on her underwear and a pair of shorts and shirt she retrieves from her backpack. "I suppose it has, hasn't it? But fortunately, we're putting it back where it belongs."

"Look, it was wrong of me to put it that way. I apologize for that. I've enjoyed the—"

"Please don't give me the 'it was nice while it lasted' speech, okay? I just don't want to hear it. We both knew that this wasn't going to last, and now it's over. I sincerely hope that you discover what happened to your godfather, Tate. And I also hope you do that without Lachlan hurting you or your friends. But I'm removing myself from the situation. You got what you wanted; once we return to the ship, I'm taking my gear and moving on."

I watch, feeling a little sick, as she hurriedly packs up the rest of her belongings. "I don't want to end it this way."

She cinches her pack tight, and then slowly turns to look at me, her expression sad. "It's too late; you already did."

CHAPTER SIXTEEN

SCHILLER

Bentley and Made don't comment as Pippa silently removes her gear from the ship and walks away without a single word other than a solemn goodbye. Not as it happens. Not the day after. Nor in the following week. They must sense my frustration and disappointment in how it all ended, but neither dares to comment on how irritated I've been since the moment she left.

That is, until the night before our last dive.

"Dude, you should just call her. This perpetual moping doesn't help anything, and it's obvious you like her."

I glare at Bentley. "I don't have her number."

He gapes at me. "You don't have her number? Don't you have any game at all?"

"There wasn't much time to get it when we were yelling at each other," I snap.

"Whoa," says Bentley. "You keep telling yourself that, I guess."

I don't bother replying. What is there to say? The last week on this ship has been dismal without her. The rest of the crew acts like they've lost a mascot, Lachlan is still on the warpath about her having quit unexpectedly, and even Made has been quieter than usual.

And then there's me, regretting every second that she's been gone. Hating how things ended between us. Is she still in Bali? Has she moved on to another island in Indonesia? Christ, what if she left the country entirely? I'll probably never see her again in my life, and every night all I do is stare up at the ceiling and wish I was staring up at her instead as she rides me until we're both gasping for air.

Some part of me wonders if it was really worth it. Was keeping Lachlan away from where I think the wreck might be located so important? I never stop wondering what might have happened between us? Am I ever going to stop wishing I could touch her one last time, hear the sound of her voice as she laughs against my chest?

Eventually. But I fear it will be a long time coming.

"I have her number."

"What?" I cry at Made.

Bentley frowns. "Dude, took you long enough to offer that little tidbit of information. He's been miserable for like a week."

Made ignores Bentley and focuses his attention on me. "She gave it to me when she said goodbye. But what did you expect, Schiller? You both clearly had an argument that ended in her leaving—something I'm glad she did, since she's now safe—and you also obviously upset her. And you think I would just give you a way to contact her? Why on earth would you believe I'd do such a thing?"

Because I need to see her again, I think but don't have the balls to admit to Made.

Nevertheless, he seems to still guess what I'm thinking because he softens and pulls his phone out of his pocket. "Here it is. Don't hurt her again or I'll come after you. She and I looked out for each other on this boat, and I feel responsible for her. She doesn't deserve any of these things that have happened."

"You don't have to worry about her with me," I say.

He gives me a considering look. "Apologize for whatever it is you said to her, and I might just believe you."

I take his phone and plug her number into mine, my hands slightly shaking, floored by the fact that I will be able to see her when I thought that would never be possible again.

"I still can't believe you made me return to the boat of a known criminal," Bentley grumbles. "My parents are going to kill me."

"I didn't make you do anything," I growl.

Bentley rolls his eyes. "Of course you did, Schill. You were clearly determined to go, and I wasn't going to just let you waltz back on here alone. I had absolutely no choice and you know it. I left two—*two*, Schiller—models in my hotel room to come here with you. Again. That's a sacrifice, man."

Made gives him a disgusted face but remains silent. I flip my friend off; Bentley's one of the most selfish people

I've ever met. If he really wanted to stay balls-deep inside those models while I returned to Lachlan, he would have.

"This might've been a waste of time, anyway," I mutter, handing Made his phone.

Bentley frowns. "How so?"

I shrug. "I mean, have *you* seen any indication that the rumors are true? I don't know about you, but I'm not exactly tripping over guns, here. There's been no hint of anything untoward. Tomorrow is our last dive before heading back to Bali, and we've found nothing. Not the wreck. Not a bunch of weapons. Certainly not any arms dealers to go with them. This whole thing might have been blown out of proportion."

And if that's true, I ended it with Pippa for no reason. Even now, she could be sitting here with us, laughing after a full day of diving before sneaking into my room later to fuck me senseless.

Made shrugs under my accusing stare. "I wouldn't be so certain. Many things are easy to hide, especially if you have the motivation. You just need to know where to look."

"Like where?"

He shrugs again. "I don't know. But I know there are hidden compartments aboard that lend all kinds of room for storing illicit goods. It's not like you're going to open the closet in your cabin and find them just waiting for you."

Bentley's eyes narrow. "How would you know that?"

"Simple logic," Made says. "All smuggler's boats are going to have hidden compartments, whether that's for drugs, guns, women, you name it."

"You seem to know a lot about it," says Bentley.

I hate to agree with him, but I do.

"My father designed some of them, okay! Is that what you were waiting to hear?" Made says, exasperated. "How else do you think my father found out about Alastair's real business and decided to quit? He had spent years customizing yachts before he was hired by Alastair.

"He soon realized what the compartments could be used for, then overheard Alastair talking about it to one of his employees. My father's been spooked for years, and now here I am, working on the damn boat he customized! It's got my father's detailing all over it. I *know*. I shouldn't even be here because of the risk, but Schiller insisted."

"Hey, this isn't my fault," I snap. "I'm seeing the situation through. If Lachlan were to find the wreck, he'd be able to do incalculable damage with what he found. I'm not going to have that on my conscience.

"But even though your father did modifications on this boat," I add, "there still haven't been any deals. No one has tried to exit or board this craft since we returned. Believe me; I've been looking."

"That's true," Bentley muses.

"No, there haven't," Made says unhappily. "I wish there were; this all could be behind us if there had. We'd be on our way back by now, you could go find Pippa, Bentley could go back to his models, and my father could finally relax knowing his son is no longer working for a terrible man."

We lapse into silence at that. It's night now and instead

of turning on the deck lights or even retiring to our cabins, we've just continued talking in the deepening darkness. I can barely see the two of them; it lends a fitting eeriness to our topic of discussion.

"Do you think that Pippa will—"

"This is the final time, Lachlan!" someone yells.

Bentley doesn't finish his sentence as we glance in the direction of the shout. Lachlan and another man are creeping down the deck, virtually invisible in the poor light.

"I assure you, this *is* the last time," Lachlan replies. "We're almost done; if he can't find it, no one can, okay? And once he's gone, I'll go back and blow the rest of it out of the water. Not that there's much left. There will be absolutely no trace, nothing to link—"

"Silence! Not out here."

"What the hell are they talking about?" Bentley whispers.

I squint through the darkness, faintly making out Lachlan and his associate, Alastair—a squatty, arrogant, nasty little fucker I loathed on sight—moving toward Lachlan's cabin.

"They must be talking about the wreck," says Made.

"Where the fuck did they come from?" I say softly. "There's no room off the bow for them to have been hiding. What the fuck?"

Alastair and Lachlan continue moving down the deck. "I don't want assurances, Lachlan. I want promises. This situation has gone on long enough. Almost thirty fucking years!"

Something cold slides down my spine. This is no idle conversation about the wreck.

"I'm going to follow them," I whisper, silently rising from my chair.

"Christ, Schiller, are you insane?" Bentley hisses.

"They're talking about my godfather like they *knew him*," I snap back. "I'm going."

Made stands as well. "I'll come, too."

"Fuuuuck, now I have to, also," says Bentley.

We creep along behind them, trying to remain silent as Lachlan and Alastair continue fighting. The rest of the yacht is quiet, the crew and dive team either asleep or in their quarters. Once they reach Lachlan's stateroom, they go inside and slam the door shut, but their voices are still audible through the door.

"You told me that Tate wouldn't be able to find it," Alastair says.

"No, I said if he couldn't, then no one would. He's got far more motivation than anyone else; if he can't find it, then inevitably others will stop looking. And anyone who doesn't will be persuaded not to—just like Tate."

"If you hadn't fucked up to begin with, none of this would have been a problem. You've put my organization at risk for nearly three decades now. I should shoot you myself and be done with it."

"That's not necessary," says Lachlan with a hint of desperation in his voice. "I'm telling you; no one was around to witness the explosion. The boat went down without a single mishap. No one has ever found it because there's nothing to be found. The entire vessel got blown out of existence, and Galvan along with it. Everyone thinks it sank—you and I know that's not true. Nothing can come back on you. I took care of Galvan like you asked. Nothing's changed. This whole expedition has been a waste of everyone's time."

There's a long pause, then Alastair says, "When I told you to get rid of Galvan, I didn't mean to do it in the most conspicuous fucking way possible. The whole world refuses to forget the miserable bastard! That's the opposite of what I wanted."

"And look how it turned out! No one even suspects foul play. A man that wealthy, disappearing any other way would have been suspicious. Thanks to me, the world just thinks he fucked up something on the boat and it sank. The damn treasure is even more of a distraction. It was perfect. You're afraid something will blow back on you that will never happen. If there's anything left, it's many feet below the surface of the ocean. Nearly impossible to find."

"Oh God," I moan. Bentley hisses at me to be quiet but I'm too overwhelmed by the revelation to pay him any mind.

Those bastards actually *murdered* him. It wasn't an accident at all. All these years I've been thinking something went wrong, that he spent his last moments on this earth terrified knowing he was going to die.

Did he wake before the ship blew? Or did he die instantly, never knowing he was marked for death, unable to save himself? I'm not sure which is worse.

Why did they kill him at all? How did Galvan know them in the first place? I was so young at the time, but I have no recollection of him ever mentioning a man from Australia.

And why would he be involved with an arms dealer in the first place! That wasn't the man I knew, the father I wished I had instead of my real one. Have I been wrong about everything all these years? Was my godfather a criminal, too? Have I been idolizing a man who never deserved it?

My mind instinctively rejects the idea. Everything I've done, the entire purpose of my life for the last decade, couldn't have been for nothing. For a man no better than a common criminal.

The door is suddenly wrenched back. Lachlan stands in the doorway, a displeased look on his face. He's holding a gun in his hand, pointed directly at my chest.

"I see I'll have to kill you now, then."

CHAPTER SEVENTEEN

PIPPA

I linger in Bali for a week. The healthier thing to do would be to move on to another island, but I just can't bring myself to do it. Not until I know that Tate, Made, and even Bentley are safe and that they've managed to return to shore, done with Lachlan for good. While I have no intention of ever speaking to him again, it will still be obvious when that massive yacht returns. Once I know they've returned I can finally turn the page on the last couple weeks.

Not that I want to.

Not that I don't miss him.

And definitely not that I wish I had been able to convince him to stay.

God, what if he's hurt? What if that asshole Lachlan is selling guns right now and figured out that Tate knows? Would Bentley and Made's presence be enough to deter him from doing something terrible?

Something makes me doubt that.

Is there anything else I could have done? Something I could have said to convince him the risk wasn't worth it? Each day I run over that final confrontation in my mind, replaying it and wondering if he might have changed his mind had I said something different at each turn.

The fact of the matter is that I'm never going to know. Not until I see that boat will I be able to relax—or move on.

"You seem more upset than usual," says Wayan.

I glance over at him. We're both sitting at our favorite table, coffees in hand, pretending not to address the elephant in the room.

I shrug. "We were only supposed to be out for about another week. Tomorrow should be their last dive before they start the return trip. And if they don't ..."

Neither of us bother finishing the thought.

Thank God I don't have to go through this alone. After I retrieved my belongings from Lachlan's boat and watched it sail away, throat tight, I took a taxi back to where Wayan found me that day. I found him at a cafe across the street from the hostel that kicked me out and said that I wanted to pay him for having driven me all across the island.

He refused, of course.

Instead, he sat me right down in the cafe and insisted I tell him the whole story. By the time I finished recounting everything that had happened—along with the suspicions Made had told Tate, who'd told me—he declared that I would stay with him until the boat returned. He'd wait for his son to return safely while I wait for Tate.

Every day one of us heads over to Sanur to see if there is any news. With each passing day with no word, it becomes harder for both of us to remain positive.

"Perhaps you should head to the port early," says Wayan, expression tight.

I shrug again. "What would be the point? It's still too early for them to have returned. I won't learn anything."

"That's likely," Wayan admits. "But you never know. Perhaps you'll meet someone else, a friend who could distract you while you wait."

"What I should do is find another job," I say.

"Is that so?"

"I should begin the process of moving on to another place. I'd originally intended to spend some time diving here, but after everything that's happened, it's the last thing I feel like doing. And if I don't want to dive, I might as well find some job that could keep me distracted in the meantime. Get paid. I have a nice cushion now from the first half of Lachlan's trip, but it wouldn't hurt to grow it. Once I figure out where to go next, I can take plenty of time off for diving."

Wayan studies me so quietly for so long it reminds me of his son. "If that's what you feel you need to do, then you should do that."

I wince. "I didn't mean to make that seem as if I'm not enjoying my time here. I'm so grateful to you for letting me stay. It's just that, even if they come back fine, I'm still going to have to ... get over him."

"You don't think you could change his mind?"

"I'm not even sure I want to. We're so different and he lied to me."

"From where I sit," says Wayan, "you have many similarities. And while a lie of omission is still a lie, who among us doesn't have things we'd prefer not to share, especially when we're lost in the first stages of love?"

"I'm not in love with him."

He says nothing.

"I'm not," I mumble, hoping it's true. But it's difficult to make myself believe that; if I felt nothing for the man, I wouldn't care so much about his safety right now.

"I guess I will head to Sanur," I mumble. "See if there's anyone hiring in the next week or two. Getting something lined up ahead of time will make it easier."

"I'll be here," says Wayan. "Text me if you need anything. I'm still waiting on Made's text today."

"Me too," I say. "I'm sure he'll text soon. They're probably just going into the water now for the morning dive. I'll see you later, okay?"

"Yes, of course."

Heading to the motorbike I've rented for the week, I climb on and head for the port. An hour and a half later, I lock my bike near the docks and begin canvassing the area yet again for a job, feeling a sad sense of deja vu. By this point in the week most of the ships have already departed, so it isn't surprising when I don't find much in the way of work, apart from a man who does day trips out for recreational divers. I'm so bored and frustrated—not to mention upset—that I nearly take him up on his offer.

However, what I need is something longer term. A few weeks, maybe even a month on some boat, sailing wherever they want to go. The farther away, the better.

There's just no one hiring.

I've very nearly resigned myself to giving up for the day when a mid-sized yacht pulls in from a mooring out in the bay. The gangway is slowly lowered once the vessel has docked, and I'm just about to head over there to see if they need any help, when out steps Andrew Lawrence.

I gape. What is *with* this guy? That's three times now I've run into him. Bali's not a huge island, but it's not *that* small, either. Enough is enough. I'm getting to the bottom of this. I march up the dock, standing at the end of the gangway, arms folded over my chest.

He halts when he sees me. "Ms. Turner? Why, what a coincidence. But I thought—shouldn't you—where's your friend? Tate, right?"

"I think you and I need to have a little chat," I say flatly.

He stares at me, something passing over his face that I haven't a hope of deciphering. "As you wish, Ms. Turner. I was just about to step out for lunch; would you care to join me?"

"Sure. That would be lovely," I say, my tone hinting it's anything but.

Andrew studies me again. "I think perhaps it would be better to have lunch aboard."

"I'm not sure I trust you enough for that."

He blinks, then says slowly, "We can stay out on my

deck. You'll be visible from the street. If you feel uncomfortable, all you'll have to do is scream."

I consider it, then decide he's right. "Fine."

He steps back, waves out a hand invitingly. "Welcome aboard, then."

I stalk up the gangway, trying to ignore how rude I'm being, but intuition demands I figure out why this guy is everywhere.

Andrew leads me over to the lounge area on deck, which, like the rest of the boat, is smaller than Lachlan's but nicer in an understated way. He pulls out my chair for me and then pushes it in once I'm ready, the casual elegance with which he does it beginning to make me question whether such a graceful man could really be that terrible.

He settles in at the other end of the table, signals for one of his crew to prepare the meal, then turns to me.

"I must confess I'm surprised to see you here," he says. "It was my understanding that you would be rejoining Lachlan's boat. Or has it already returned? It should any day now, yes?"

"And how do you know that?"

"Everyone knows that. Lachlan's comings and goings are well-known to anyone who's lived here for a significant period of time."

"Well, that's convenient," I say. "Maybe then you can tell me why you've been following me and Tate around."

"Whatever do you mean?" Andrew says innocently.

I glare at him. "Don't give me that. You and I both know you coincidentally showing up wherever we were was no coincidence at all. I want to know how you're involved with this expedition, and I want to know now. And if you don't tell me, I'll call the authorities here and have them go out and *get* that boat. I don't care who Lachlan thinks he is. I'm tired of worrying whether Schiller will ever get off that ..." I'm unable to finish, nausea making my stomach clench.

Andrew's eyes widen. "You care about Tate, don't you?" he whispers.

"Of course I do. Anyone would when the man running the show is clearly—"

"No, Ms. Turner," he says softly. "You *care* for him. You love him, yes?"

I rub the edge of the table with my index finger, eyes cast downward. What is it about older people who believe their age gives them the right to ask impertinent questions?

But Andrew remains silent, calmly waiting for me to reply until I finally begrudgingly say, "I seem to. Or at least, I could, perhaps. Despite everything."

"Or perhaps because of everything."

I grumble something in the affirmative, but when I finally glance up, something flashes in Andrew's eyes I could swear is happiness. And that doesn't make any sense. Why would he care?

He leans toward me. "I am going to tell you something, Ms. Turner. Something that would get both of us in great trouble if it ever got out that I told you."

"Then by all means, don't feel obligated," I say quickly, although this is exactly what I want.

"Based on your relationship with Tate—because you

love him—I feel it's relevant, even necessary, for you to know."

"I'm not sure I understand—"

"Miles Lachlan is an arms dealer."

"I know."

Andrew looks shocked. "How?"

"Made—one of the locals—told Tate, who told me."

"Ah. That would explain it. And did Made tell you anything else?"

"Just that there might have been arms shipments on board with us."

"Quite. So you have the large of it, but you still need the remaining details."

"Why are you telling me this?" I ask. "I get that I came in here demanding to know why you kept popping up around us, but why actually tell me?"

"My reasons for doing so shall become apparent in the telling, my dear."

"Okay ..."

"Ah yes. So where were we? I suppose I'll begin at the start. Thirty years ago, or rather, just about three decades ago, Lachlan met Lawrence Galvan."

"Really?" I gasp. "So he *is* involved."

Andrew nods. "Oh yes. He very much is. At the time, Galvan and Tate's family were looking to expand their shipping lanes in Oceania. Lachlan approached Galvan and said that he could use his connections, grease the wheels, that sort of thing. The market collapse in '90 had worsened by the following year, and the company had particular exposure to Japan as well, whose economy was imploding. Suddenly Galvan and Tate's parents found themselves in a precarious situation.

"When Lachlan approached Galvan, he thought the answers to their problems had been solved. They could pivot to Oceania, ride out the recession, and once things had stabilized, they'd continue their regular routes from Asia to America."

"I'm guessing that didn't happen."

"Oh, it did," Andrew says. "Other things just *also* happened."

"I'm assuming some guns hitched a ride in some of those shipping containers?"

"You assume correctly. This went on for, oh, a little over a year? The Tates never found out, but Galvan did, and he was so furious he actually confronted Lachlan about it."

I wince. "What I've come to know about Lachlan tells me he didn't take too kindly to that."

"No, he did not. Sensing his place in the criminal empire was in jeopardy—even then, Lachlan was never the head honcho—he tried to kill Galvan right then, but Galvan managed to escape. Knowing that his life was in danger and wanting to keep the Tates out of it—especially their little son—Galvan fled on his ship. But he was only a few days out from Bali when it went down."

"So where do you come in?" I ask in confusion.

He sighs. "Interpol has been trying to take down this arms network for many, many years. They've got enough to link Lachlan to a bunch of sales in this area, but they still need him with the smoking gun, so to speak. This expedition he's on supposedly will give them that. Apparently, some deal is going down aboard. And I've been helping Interpol assemble enough evidence to bring Lachlan to justice."

"Why? Why you?"

"I knew the Tates," he says after a long moment. "It's been a while since we've met, since I live here and they're based in the US, but I always liked them. My connections are particularly deep in this part of the world, so I offered my assistance to Interpol."

"And they took it?"

"They did."

"We need to do something to stop this deal! Tate, Made, even Bentley could get caught between the two parties. It isn't safe for any of them. Why are you just sitting here when we could be putting a stop to it?"

Andrew's jaws clench. "What do you think I've been doing? The reason I've been following you, as you put it, is because Interpol didn't want any of you on that boat when the final showdown occurred. We wanted you well out of the way, since it's heavily suspected that Galvan's wreck wasn't an accident, that Lachlan sabotaged the vessel. So I, being the harmless old man that I am, decided to warn you off before going back. Against orders, I might add. I'm not supposed to be inserting myself deliberately into the situation. Apparently, despite the risk of getting in trouble, I was only half successful."

I stare at him, trying to digest all that he's just told me and failing miserably.

"So ... that's it? You're trying to catch the man who murdered Galvan? And it's taken nearly thirty years to find any evidence that Lachlan killed him?"

Andrew pauses, expression trying to telegraph something to me. "No, Ms. Turner. I'm not trying to solve Galvan's murder. I *am* Lawrence Galvan."

CHAPTER EIGHTEEN

SCHILLER

"Whoa, hey, stop," Bentley says to Lachlan, squeezing my arm and uselessly trying to drag me back.

Lachlan glares at him. "I have the gun and *you're* the one giving orders? I think not. Come inside, gentlemen. We wouldn't want the rest of the crew to overhear what you just have, yes?"

"As if they aren't already part of your *special* organization," says Made.

Lachlan shrugs. "That's true; they're my employees, after all. But the dive team isn't. Would you like me to add their bodies to the bottom of the ocean along with yours?"

"You can't actually kill us," I say. "Everyone will know something's wrong. You'll be the prime suspect. You can't be that stupid."

Lachlan's eyes narrow; he throws a glance over his

shoulder at Alastair, as if embarrassed the people he's threatening aren't quaking in their boots.

"But you're wrong," he says, turning back to us. "Who better to deliver the message of the tragic, tragic dive accident than the other divers?"

"If that's the case," I snap, "then you can't exactly shoot us, can you? That gun's no threat. Besides, what are they going to think, that we decided to take a midnight dive?"

"It's not much of a stretch. But sure, why risk it? I'll just tell them tomorrow morning you decided to go ahead of them. When you never come out of the water, oh dear. So tragic. Problem solved."

"Experienced divers would never believe that. They stick to their dive plan, which includes me," I say.

"Even I know that," says Bentley. "And I'm a shitty diver."

Lachlan's face turns dark. "Well, if you'd just died that day like you were supposed to, then I wouldn't have had to come up with an alternate plan on the fly! But instead, that woman saved you and—"

"*You* sabotaged the O-ring?" I say sharply.

Lachlan sneers. "Of course I did. And it would have been a *brilliant* accident, too. So simple. We could have ended this bullshit weeks ago. But no. She saved you, and then we had to keep up the charade for weeks. You were already supposed to be dead by the time Alastair arrived. If only you'd—"

"Enough of this," Alastair interrupts. "Kill them and be done with it. And you better be correct that no one else will ever find the wreck site because I'm ready to wash my hands of this mess. You assured me there would be nothing to find thirty years ago, and now here we are, having to deal with Tate."

"It's fine," says Lachlan. "He's the only one who really cares about it. The sole person who keeps looking. That wreck's a novelty to everyone else; no one even seriously looked for it until Tate came onto the scene all those years later, publicly proclaiming he thought it could be found. That's why I've told you that you don't need to worry about anything that's left. There's nothing that could be linked back to you. Tate's the only one who's a problem. And once he horrifically dies trying to find it, no one else will want to go looking. Some treasures simply aren't worth the risk."

"Except it won't be that simple," I say.

Alastair shoves Lachlan out of the way. "And why the fuck not?"

"Because," I say, smiling grimly, "I already know that we aren't anywhere near the wreck site. I've been deliberately moving you away from it."

Alastair goes apoplectic. "You little shit!" He wheels on Lachlan. "You told me he didn't know the location!"

"He's bluffing! He doesn't have a damn clue! I've been letting him lead us around by the nose, knowing that I'll have all the time in the world to go back and clean up the rest of it after he's dead."

"But I do, though. I know exactly where it is," I say, lying through my teeth. I've spent so much time on the ocean floor in this area that I have a pretty good idea of the few spots left where it could be, but I'm not sure yet of the exact location. "And I've already passed on that information to my parents. They loved Galvan so much as well, you know. What are you going to do, arrange their deaths as well, all the way across the world? My death, you might be able to explain away, but theirs, too? Highly suspicious."

Alastair's face turns red even as Lachlan's pales. Bentley's head whips toward me, but he wisely remains silent, knowing I'm completely talking out of my ass right now. What other choice do I have? If they think someone off this ship also knows about their little skeleton in the deep, then they'll be forced to think twice about killing us, knowing it would always be linked back to them.

"You told me this would end the situation!" Alastair yells. "You said this would fix it. Instead, you've made it worse, yet again! This is what I should have done years ago."

Alastair pulls a phone out of his pocket and dials a number, says "Get in here," then hangs up. A second later, two armed guards I've never seen before barge into the room.

"Whoa," says Bentley, backing away from them. "You guys are fucking huge."

"And you would do well to shut up about them if you don't want them to throw you overboard," Alastair snaps. "I don't care how many railroad cars your family owns, Bentley."

Bentley pales. "Hey, what the—how do you—"

"Know who you are? Please, your family runs the

largest private railroad in the United States, and you thought I wouldn't recognize the crest on the ring you always wear? It's my job to know which families move goods around the world, boy."

"What the fuck does that mean?"

"It means I'm a big fan of your little railroad. I'm what you would call a frequent customer."

Bentley pales even further. "You're saying my family *works* with you?"

Alastair smiles nastily. Even I feel my face draining of color. Made remains silent next to me, his eyes tracking around the room, cataloguing every single movement.

"That's not true!" Bentley cries. "We wouldn't work with criminals like you, you lying sack of shit."

Alastair rolls his eyes. "I suggest you begin investigating where that inheritance of yours really comes from, instead of just blowing it all on booze and women."

He dismisses Bentley and returns his attention to Lachlan. Snapping his fingers at the guards, he says, "Take his gun and detain him in his cabin until I decide what to do about this situation."

"Wait, you don't need to do that!" Lachlan says. "This has gotten out of hand. I know I'm right. Tate is bluffing. He doesn't have a damn clue where the wreck is. We can still kill them and be done with it!"

"Perhaps, but as is usual with you, that would necessitate it being done messily, and I prefer cleanliness myself."

Alastair motions to his goons. They grab Lachlan, disarm him, and give the gun to Alastair, then drag him from the room over Lachlan's vehement protests. Silence falls once they leave. Alastair turns back to us, leveling the gun at me.

"Now what to do about you?"

"I vote you let us go," Bentley says.

Alastair sneers. "Now why would I do that?"

"Perhaps you could consider doing it as a personal favor to my parents," Bentley says bitterly. I glance at him sharply; we'll need to have a discussion about what Alastair's just told him about his parents, but right now, we can't afford for him to understandably fall to pieces.

Sharing a look with Made, I nod subtly behind Alastair. He nods back in assent and begins slowly edging his way behind him. If I can distract him long enough, the three of us should be able to incapacitate Alastair before he has a chance to do anything to us. And we need to do it now, before his guards return and the odds are still in our favor.

"So you're the man who killed my godfather," I say, walking over to the bar and pouring myself a drink, which conveniently gets Alastair to turn toward me, thus giving his back to Made.

"I'm the man who ordered it, via Lachlan. Obviously, I didn't kill him myself." Alastair says flatly.

"Obviously," I say, not bothering to keep the sarcasm from my tone. "Whatever did he do to earn the execution order?"

Alastair shrugs. "What else? He dared to assume he could just back out of our agreement."

"In other words, he declined to continue facilitating crime, and you killed him for it."

"If that's how you need to think of it, I certainly won't stop you," says Alastair impassively. "But even criminals have contracts. It's not all shoot-outs and backstabbing. Should I have no recourse when a man reneges on his agreement?"

I take a long sip of the bourbon, feeling the liquor burn down my throat. What awful irony. Here I am, finally discovering what happened to Galvan and all I feel is exhausted. Horribly sad that this is how it ended for him. There will be no wreck to find; I'm sure the entire boat was blown to smithereens precisely for that reason. Everything I've worked for this last decade was pointless.

Thank Christ Pippa isn't here. She could have been. Had just a few things happened differently, she might be standing here next to me now; a gun pointed in her face instead of mine. I shudder.

If I get off this boat, I'm going to find her. I don't care how long it takes or how far I have to travel to track her down, I'm going to apologize for the nasty things we said and never let her go until she realizes how much she means to me.

Because she was right. It *wasn't* worth it.

"So is that what this trip was supposed to be?" I ask. "One final clean-up of all the loose ends? Or was Lachlan also selling guns right under our noses?"

Alastair shrugs. "In all honesty, I would have let it go if you hadn't kept pushing. While I'd never admit it to Lachlan's face because I can extract more profit from him by keeping him afraid of me, I wasn't entirely concerned about someone finding the wreck until you came along. That conviction only grew as years passed and no one found even a hint of it. Then you became obsessed with finding it.

"At first, we thought you would give up like the others—spoiled rich brat, getting frustrated that he didn't immediately find what he was looking for, et cetera—but you kept pushing. And getting closer. You may or may not have stumbled upon the actual location, but I can no longer afford the risk of letting you discover it. Thus I made Lachlan hire you for a little trip.

"And yes, killing two birds with one stone is always most efficient," he continues. "There have indeed been a few deals conducted while you were sleeping. Then you were supposed to be silenced and the problem finally concluded."

"You must know I'm not going to just let that happen," I say, fist tightening around my glass.

"Well, I certainly wouldn't expect you to take it lying down. Unfortunately for you, it's unlikely you'll be successful. You're never getting off this ship alive. And whatever happened to the woman who saved you? Where did she go?"

"She has nothing to do with this," I snap, terrified he might retaliate against her. "She had a disagreement with one of the other divers and decided not to continue after we returned to Bali."

"Is that so? Judging by your concerned expression, I

rather think not. Something tells me there's a bit more to that story, Mr. Tate. Tell me, did you tell her any of your suspicions before you left her? Pillow talk can have surprisingly dangerous repercussions, you know."

"You won't get near her," I growl. "I'll stop you before you can."

"It's admirable you think so," says Alastair. He straightens his suit jacket and slips the gun inside an interior pocket. "In any case, I have a deal to get back to. I'll just lock you inside this room until there's time to deal with you. Enjoy your remaining hours on earth; it's important to be grateful for—"

Sudden shouts ring out from the deck outside, followed by the sound of gunfire and footsteps sprinting along the deck. Bentley and I whirl toward the door, expecting it to come crashing in at any moment.

"I think I've heard quite enough," Made suddenly says.

We turn to him. Made is standing before Alastair, a gun pointed directly at him.

"What the hell?" says Bentley, throwing up his hands.

"Where did you get that gun?" Alastair barks, reaching into his suit jacket.

"I wouldn't do that if I were you," Made growls. "You'll be dead before you can draw. Now get on the ground and put your hands behind your head."

"Made? What the fuck is going on here?"

"That's what I'd like to know," Bentley mutters, hands still raised. Made ignores him, still staring at Alastair.

"Give me that gun this instant, and I'll grant you a quick death," Alastair screeches, sweat visible on his brow.

"That won't be happening. Can't you hear how quiet it's become? Your guards can't save you now."

My head jerks toward the door. He's right; the boat *is* silent, eerily quiet, in fact. Alastair throws an uneasy glance at the door himself, and when none of his guards barge in, all the fight leaks out of him.

Made smiles, his gun unwavering. "That deal you just had to get back to? It wasn't with a syndicate out of Java. We're actually Interpol. And you, Bretton Alastair, are under arrest."

CHAPTER NINETEEN

PITT

The call finally comes in the middle of the night. Galvan and I both sprint for it, but naturally I, by virtue of being much younger, outpace him.

"Made?" I cry.

"Pippa? Yes, I'm here," he says, voice as calmly quiet as ever.

"Well? What happened? Did you catch Lachlan and his boss? Is ... did Schiller find out before? Is he okay? Please tell me he's all right!"

"Judging by the fact that you answered his phone, I'm going to assume you're with Andrew right now?" he says dryly.

I flinch. Oh shit. I'm not supposed to know Galvan is really alive, that he's been living under his middle name, Andrew, since his faked death, but in my anxiety, I completely forgot. My eyes fly to Galvan, who is wincing himself but still waves at me to continue. I put the phone on speaker and say, "I ... ran into him again at the port and we decided to have lunch."

"And is lunch now after twelve o'clock at night?"

I don't have an answer for that.

"You know who he really is, don't you."

Oh shit. Now we're really in for it. "I ... guessed it."

"Really. You guessed the man who's been dead for thirty years was really alive all along?"

"And faked his death to help you catch an arms cartel? Yeah ... I guessed that as well," I say lamely. Throughout the day, Galvan has filled me in on all the details—that he went to Interpol to alert the authorities to what he'd discovered, their assurances that they could protect him, his decision to fake his own death to avoid Alastair going after the Tates, and his anguish over doing it to Schiller. The whole thing.

And what an incredible story! But he wasn't supposed to tell me any of it, so I might as well just take responsibility for the leak myself. It'll take some of the heat off Galvan. If that allows Schiller to meet him that much sooner, then so much the better.

"Perhaps I should recruit you myself, with those kinds of deductive capabilities," Made says, his tone more sarcastic than I've ever heard it.

"This is ridiculous," Galvan suddenly says. "While appreciated, my dear, I won't let you take the blame for me. Yes, Made, obviously I told her myself. She was beside herself and the entire world will know in a few weeks, anyway. Assuming you caught the bastards, that is?"

"Yes, we caught them. All of them."

"Then the time for secrecy has passed. Schiller would have told her, anyway. Or do you expect me to still keep my identity hidden from him?"

"I suppose there's no reason for that," Made says slowly. "Unofficially, anyway. If word leaks about you coming back from the grave before we call you to testify, then I will come for you myself. Your existence needs to stay a secret until the trial. I know all about your little coincidental run-ins with Pippa at that waterfall and restaurant, by the way. I *told* you it wasn't safe for you to make contact and that I was watching out for both of them. If someone had identified you—anyway, just don't tell anyone else on my team. I don't want to have to write that report. I'm covering for both of you, and that's because I trust you, got it?"

"I can't believe you're a damn Interpol agent," I say. "You lied to me the whole time. And to think I actually felt I had to protect you when Lachlan tried to fire you!"

"I actually truly appreciated that, Pippa," says Made softly. "Although it was completely unnecessary, considering I'd already been assigned undercover to the yacht and you were in way over your head. But you were also always kind to my father. Which is why I'm covering for you now by not reporting to my superiors that you know who Andrew really is."

"Does your dad know?"

"He knows I work for the government, but not Interpol specifically. I was a teenager when he barely managed to escape with his life from Alastair's employ; I decided right then that I would be the one to bring them down. And now

I finally have. But I can't tell him any specifics, and he respects that. Which is surely why when he noticed that you were joining a crew of a boat I was on, he advised you to stay away."

"He made it seem like you always work on boats."

"And that's because I do. They serve as useful covers for my work, and I happen to enjoy diving."

"Hmm," I say.

"When can we see Schiller," Galvan says impatiently.

"They're interviewing him now. Along with Bentley. I imagine it's going to take most of the night. By the time they release them, they'll likely want to sleep it off. But I'll be sure to point him in your direction, Pippa."

"Mine?" I squeak, noticing the crestfallen expression on Galvan's face.

"Officially, I can't send him to Andrew, remember?" Made says, which makes Galvan brighten. "But Tate wants to see you anyway, and if you just so happen to be staying on a boat with a particular person ..."

"Then what an amazing coincidence that would be," says Galvan with satisfaction.

"He's already got your number, Pip," says Made, causing my gut to clench with nerves. "I'm sure it won't be long before he shows up. I've got to go; there's a lot to be done to start processing these people."

"Thank you, Made," Galvan says. "For everything."

"The work is only now beginning," he says, before hanging up.

Galvan and I stare at each other in stunned silence. He slowly sinks back down into his chair.

"I can't believe I'm going to see him tomorrow ... after all these years. Do you ... how do you think he's going to take it?"

I wince. "Being totally honest?"

He nods.

"I think he's going to be pissed. He hates being coddled, and when he realizes you left him alone his entire life to protect him, he's going to be angry. He'll then get over it, and even understand—he was a defenseless kid, after all, and who knows what Alastair might have done?—but until he does ... yeah."

"I suppose you're right," he sighs. "And that's how it should be; I'd never want him to let people manipulate him. I just still think of him as that little boy, you know? He was barely four when I ... when it happened. Even though I've watched his life from afar, I feel as though I don't know him at all."

"You will," I say firmly. "And we're going to sit here all night if necessary, to figure out how to make that happen."

"PIPPA?"

"Up here!" I call from the deck. Galvan and I stare at each other. "This is it. Are you ready?"

"To come back from the dead? As ready as one can be on such an occasion."

I get up from my chair and move away from the table. "Okay, remember what we talked about. Let me ease him into it. With you sitting under the umbrella and wearing that hat, he's not going to recognize you right away if you keep your head down. We don't want to give him a heart attack, right? You've been gone for a long time."

Galvan nods. "Right. Am I the only one this nervous?"

"You're definitely not," I say, although my nervousness is for a completely different reason.

"Pippa."

I turn. Schiller is standing at the end of the deck. We drink in the sight of each other. I take in his every feature, desperately searching for any injury and only slightly relaxing once I discover none. My stomach clenches painfully; he could have *died*. How has this man come to mean so much to me in such a short time?

Schiller steps forward, and I do too, until we meet in the middle, our eyes still locked together.

"Whose boat is this?" he asks. "Never mind. It doesn't matter. What I've come to say is more important."

"But maybe first we should—"

"Just let me get this out first, okay? I'm nervous as hell and I need to say it."

"Okay," I say, throwing an apologetic glance at Galvan, whose newly shaven face is hidden in shadow. "Do you, um, want privacy for this discussion, or ...?"

Schiller blinks at me. "What?" He glances at the man sitting under the umbrella, squints at him as though he recognizes him, then shakes his head. "No, I don't care who hears. I want everyone to know, actually."

He comes closer, taking me by the shoulders and gathering me against him. "I was so wrong to say those things to you, Pippa, and I've been hating myself ever since. I said what we had wasn't a real relationship, and that was complete horseshit. Nothing has ever felt as real as being with you.

"I want us to be together so we can figure out if what we have—this *relationship*—will last. Forever. And I don't care how crazy that sounds or that we've only known each other for a few weeks. When Lachlan had that gun on me last night—"

"*What?*" I bark. "Made never said he had a gun on you!"

"—all I could think about was getting back to you, being with you, how much I regretted how we'd ended it. I swore right then that I would do anything I had to to tell that to you. And so ... yeah. That's everything. Christ, I've never made such a confession to a woman in my entire life." He plows a hand through his hair, causing it to stick up in every direction.

I gape at him. He shifts on his feet, jaws clenched. A second later, unable to take it anymore, he says, a hint of nervousness in his tone, "Well?"

I suck in a shaky breath. "Um, yeah. All of that. I'm sorry I said those things to you and regret how we ended it. And while you've been gone, each day has been unending torment wondering if you're okay. So ... yes. The answer is yes, I want to see if our relationship lasts."

Schiller crushes his mouth to mine, taking me so swiftly it's all I can do to kiss him back.

Suddenly, he pulls away. "Wait, he called you last night? But that would have been practically right after it happened. Why did he call you so soon? When did he have the time?"

Oh God. Here it comes. "It wasn't me he called, Schiller," I whisper.

Schiller squints at me. "He didn't? Then who—"

"It was me," Galvan says, standing and coming out from under the umbrella. He steps into the sunlight and removes his hat, then stares directly into Schiller's eyes.

Schiller stumbles back from me. He turns, takes one step toward Galvan, then halts as if unsure what his eyes are telling him is really possible. For one horribly long moment, there's nothing but awful silence.

And then he erupts.

"Where have you *been* the last thirty fucking years!"

"I've been with you every year of your life. Following each bit of your journey as much as I could while still keeping you safe."

Schiller emits the sound of a wounded animal. *"You left me alone in that house."*

Tears spring to Galvan's eyes. "I know. I know, son, and I've always hated it."

"But you just couldn't let me know you were alive? When I cried myself to sleep every night for months as a fucking toddler, you thought that wouldn't damage me forever?"

Galvan straightens, blinking the tears away. "What was I supposed to do, Schiller, let Lachlan get it into his head to come after your parents? How might he have done that? He would have gone after *you*. I couldn't risk that. Never.

"They had to be put away. But it's taken longer than expected. If I'd known it would take three decades to stop them, I never would have agreed to it! I would have taken you away somewhere safe."

Schiller doubles over at the waist, chest heaving like he's on the verge of hyperventilating. "I can't believe this. I can't fucking believe it. You *left* me," he says, voice wobbling.

"He only did what he thought was right, Schiller. He's suffered along with you because of it."

"And you!" he yells, shooting upright and whirling on me. "You knew, and you didn't tell me? How could you?"

"I only found out yesterday, Schiller," I say quietly. "And I didn't have your number."

"But you had Made's."

"I didn't want Andrew to get in trouble! He wasn't supposed to tell me. Nor did I want to interfere with the investigation. What if your change in behavior had tipped Lachlan off and he got away? We wouldn't be having this conversation. Do you think I'd do anything to jeopardize the moment you're having right now?"

Schiller's jaw clenches and he jerks his head. He paces

around in a tight little circle, muttering to himself. I watch with tears in my eyes, so sad for him I can hardly breathe.

After a moment that feels like forever, he sighs and his shoulders slump. "No. You're right. Last time I didn't listen to your explanation and look what happened. And had you told me, it would have been a struggle to hide it from Lachlan. By that I mean it would have been impossible not to plant a fist in his face," he adds ruefully.

Schiller stalks over to Galvan, who suddenly looks frail compared to Schiller's own vitality. Schiller stares down at him for a moment, something like disbelieving amazement in his eyes. He reaches out a hand and cradles Galvan's wizened cheek.

"I'm not going to pretend I can just get over this," Schiller says hoarsely. "It's not something a person can just accept. But I am so damn glad you're alive."

And then he folds him into a hug.

CHAPTER TWENTY

SCHILLER

THREE MONTHS LATER

I watch as my godfather takes the stand. His sudden reappearance, announced officially two weeks after the arrest of Lachlan and Alastair, set off an international media firestorm my family is still dealing with. For weeks now, anywhere my parents, Galvan, or I go, we're hounded by reporters, all hurling questions at us about the greatest comeback this decade.

The only disappointing thing about Galvan's entire story for the media is the fact that there was never any sunken treasure. Turns out he never set out from Bali on that last voyage—he just planted the rumor to attract the attention of Lachlan. His real wealth stayed sitting in his accounts the entire time, drawn down over the last three decades through shell companies that didn't tie back to him so that Lachlan wouldn't realize he was alive. If any one of us had thought to look, we might have discovered the truth long ago.

My parents were deeply shaken by Galvan's return. Once they got over their shock, like me, they welcomed him with open arms. Seeing their genuine pleasure at Galvan being alive allowed me to view our own relationship with new eyes. The three of us still aren't close, but perhaps one day there might be room for a new relationship, now that they understand the importance of being there for the people you love while they're still around.

"He doesn't look nervous," Pippa whispers next to me, interrupting my rumination over the drama of these last months.

I put my arm around her shoulder and squeeze. Someone snaps a photo from the press gallery. My eyes fly to the asshole and I glare at him; he snaps another shot and throws a thumbs-up. Pippa squeezes my knee without saying a word. Our relationship has also been fodder for the media wolves; that I'm so protective of it only makes them hungrier. I guess we provide good food for the gossip rags.

"Should I go take his camera off him once we're done here?" I whisper into her hair. The camera snaps again and I glare at him over her head a second time.

"Just ignore him. Once this whole thing is over, they'll quickly lose interest in us, anyway."

"How could someone ever grow bored of photographing you? I certainly don't."

"Schiller!" she hisses. "For God's sake, don't talk about

that now. Especially not now that they're swearing in your godfather."

Giving the reporter one last look, I turn my attention to the stand and listen as the district attorney of New York City—the case got punted to the city since that was Galvan's official domicile in 1992—begins soliciting Galvan's testimony. The courtroom listens, spellbound, as he recounts his initial meeting with Lachlan, how they worked out an agreement, and then everything after, leading up to that final night when he drove his ship out to sea, knowing it was wired to explode, and then quickly abandoning it for the Interpol boat that met him. By the time he finishes telling what it was like to watch his life explode along with the boat, there's not a dry eye in the room.

By now I've heard this story many times, both when he originally told it that day on the boat after I calmed down enough to think straight, and after, including when Galvan returned with me to meet my parents and while practicing for this very testimony. It doesn't get any easier for me to hear it, though. Pippa squeezes my knee again. I reach for her hand and intertwine our fingers.

I never would have survived any of this without her. She completely uprooted her life for me, putting traveling on hold to support me during Galvan's part in the trial and even my own. I, too, will have to testify at some point, since both Lachlan and Alastair threatened my life. The D.A. is hoping my testimony will be the one to seal the deal with these assholes.

Once the D.A. finishes, he turns it over to Lachlan's defense attorney. Alastair's trial has yet to begin; hopefully they won't cut Lachlan a deal to get Alastair a worse conviction, but something tells me after the testimony my uncle just gave, it's going to be hard to sway the jury back in Lachlan's direction. Indeed, he barely questions the man before allowing him to leave the stand. The judge calls a recess until the following day, and that's it. The security guards begin ushering people out of the room.

"That was intense," says Pippa. "Even more intense than hearing him practice it before. Something about a courtroom, huh?"

"Yeah, something," I mutter, too preoccupied by the people pushing toward us to muster a real response. "We'd better get out of here before it becomes a complete madhouse. I don't feel like giving a statement to the press, do you?"

"Definitely not."

Taking her hand in mine, I weave around the crowd, nodding to Galvan and my parents before leading Pippa out the side door.

"Whew," Pippa says. "Glad to be out of that crush."

"Well, we'd better get out of here if you want that to continue," I say, leading us quickly down the hall toward the metal detectors at the side entrance. People are already breaking out into the hallway; within moments they'll be coming this way. By that time, I want us to already be driving away.

"You just don't want to run into that reporter again."

"I don't want to run into any of them. Don't you despise your privacy being invaded like that?"

"Of course. But it's a small price to pay to draw attention to this case. You know public sentiment against Lachlan is what's going to put him behind bars."

"Yes, yes," I grumble. "We've gone over this before. Many times, in fact."

"But it appears you still need the reminder," she prods gently.

"You can give me all the reminders you want once we're in the car," I growl.

She laughs. "Why do I get the feeling that the reminders you're referring to require my lips but not my speech?"

"Because they don't," I wink, hustling us out of the courthouse and into the car I instructed our driver to have waiting here.

"You really planned out our whole escape, huh?" Pippa says once we've settled into the backseat and the driver has pulled away.

I start pulling at my tie. "I just hate the constant song and dance. Christ, I've worn a suit more times in the last three months than I have in the last decade. We should be on a boat somewhere."

"It's so weird being back here," Pippa says absently. I glance over; she's staring out the window as downtown Manhattan crawls by. Forgetting the tie, I reach over and take her hand again, giving it a reassuring squeeze.

"Have you decided what you're going to do about your

parents?" I ask quietly.

She shrugs, still staring out the window, but her hand stays tightly clutching mine. "Well, they obviously know I'm back in the US for the first extended period of time since I graduated high school. And they certainly know I'm with you, since our pictures are plastered all over the newsstands."

"But you haven't contacted them."

She remains silent for a long time, then finally says, "No, but you know they've tried. I haven't decided yet whether I'll open that door. Do you think it's ironic, me ending up with someone who, on paper, is exactly the kind of man they've always wanted for me?"

"You know it's not that simple, Pip," I say.

"Isn't it though? You're the insanely wealthy and famous person they'd love to see me with. And obviously *I* know you're more than that, but ... what does it say about me that this is how things have ended up? I literally fled to the other side of the world to escape their influence and now here I am, years later, back in New York and dating a man who will inherit not one, but two massive fortunes one day. Do they know my mind better than I do after all?"

"You fell in love with me *despite* all that," I say roughly, "not because of it."

Finally she looks at me, eyes wide. I lean closer.

"W-what did you say?" she stutters.

"You do love me, don't you?" I say, eyes never leaving hers. "Because I'm totally, completely in love with you and want to spend the rest of my life with you, Pippa Turner."

"What are you saying?" she chokes out.

"Oh, I'm not proposing anything," I say, then wink at her. "Yet. I'm not going to propose to a woman in the back of a moving vehicle."

"Right," she says weakly. "Because that would be insane."

"Pippa," I say, taking her face in my hands. "That would, of course, be dependent on one thing from you."

She smiles. "And what would that be?"

"Whether you feel the same way about me," I say, entirely certain of her answer and yet somehow still nervous to hear it.

Her smile widens. "Ah, well. Since you need to hear this, too, then you should know that I am completely, totally in love with you as well."

She kisses me, hands wrapped around my head to draw me closer to her. I kiss her back, coaxing her mouth to open for me and then deepening the kiss. In seconds, I'm pulling her across the seat and straddling her over my waist. I take her mouth again, the kiss building in intensity so quickly I'm glad for the tinted windows.

"You know," she suddenly says, tearing her mouth from mine, "there *is* something I've always wanted to do in the back of a moving vehicle, though."

I grin up at her. "And what is that?"

She laughs. "I think you know."

I pull her back to me. "I do," I say against her mouth, then press the button to raise the divider between us and the driver.

EPILOGUE

PIPPA

TEN YEARS LATER

"If we start now, we have time for a quickie before the kids wake up."

I open my eyes to discover Schiller pulling my pajama shirt over my head. Laughing, I lift up so he can pull it over my head, then wriggle my hips to kick off my sleep shorts as well. Schiller groans and drops his head between my thighs, loving me with his mouth until I'm shoving my face into the pillow to muffle the cries from my orgasm.

After I recover, I roll onto him. He's already shucked his pants and is stroking himself. I take him inside my mouth as he continues pumping up from the base of his shaft, swirling my mouth over his head as he groans low in his throat.

"Tate!" someone hisses through the door, voice thick with an Italian accent.

Schiller and I freeze. "What?" Schiller calls back, voice hoarse but remarkably steady considering the fact that his cock is still thrust down my throat.

"I got out of bed early to take care of all the kids so you can continue fucking your wife, but I expect to be extended the same courtesy tomorrow morning!" the man hisses.

Schiller barks with laughter, sending him further down my throat, before gently withdrawing and calling to the door, "You got it, Marco."

"I expect at least a full hour, Tate!" Marco hisses before the sounds of his footsteps retreat down the hall.

Schiller and I look at each other and laugh. "Well, at least now we have time," I say.

Schiller pulls me up, taking a nipple in his mouth and sucking firmly. I gasp and then bite my lower lip to keep from making another sound; the children might be temporarily distracted, but I certainly don't want them to hear us.

"I have to say, when we met Marco and Izzy on our honeymoon in Florence, I never thought we'd be together here, nearly a decade later and corralling five children between us while we sail the Mediterranean," I say drowsily as Schiller continues sucking.

Schiller releases me and lifts his head to growl, "Pippa, a man doesn't want to hear about another when he's in the middle of fucking his wife, as Marco nicely put it."

I smirk at him and grind my throbbing core against his shaft. "Even when he's the reason we can have a leisurely fuck now? When's the last time that even happened?"

"It's been two months, a week, and three days," Schiller groans. "Now put me inside you."

I burst into laughter. "Are you seriously counting?"

"You mean do I count the time between when I last lost myself in your body without interruption? Yeah. I do. Young children will do that to a husband."

Snickering, I say, "Well, I must say you've gotten *incredibly* good at getting me off real quick. In very creative ways, I might add."

"When there's only half an hour between one child getting up and the next every morning, you have to take initiative. Now for fuck's sake, *please* can you put my cock inside you? Keep grinding against me like that and I won't last a minute."

Wrapping my arms around his neck, I slowly lower myself onto his shaft, rolling my hips in small circles that have Schiller's eyes rolling back in his head. I lift up and then sink back down, grinding in a lazy rhythm that quickly has both of us softly moaning.

Schiller lets me keep riding him, his chest twitching and his hands shaking with the effort to not lose control. Suddenly gripped by the urge to tease him, I lower my head and whisper in his ear, "Something makes me think you no longer *can* do it slowly."

I'm instantly flipped onto my back, Schiller spreading my legs wide as he surges into me. He grabs my wrists and locks them over my head, then growls against my mouth, "I don't think I like what you're insinuating, wife."

"Please, please prove me wrong," I gasp against him.

Schiller's mouth descends on mine and he sets about doing just that, riding me in long, lazy strokes until many minutes later I'm begging him to let me explode. He joins me an instant later, spending inside me as I'm still pulsing around him. He rolls us onto our sides, our chests heaving as we drag air into our lungs.

"Teasing you was a very good idea," I manage a few seconds later.

He chuckles. "Whenever you need that proven to you again, you just let me know."

"Believe me, I will be doing just that," I say, then reluctantly untangle myself from him.

"Where are you going?" he says, disgruntled.

I throw a sly smile over my shoulder. "If we *really* hurry, we can also shower together."

He's out of the bed in a shot.

Once we come out onto the deck, Marco gives us a look of hideous jealousy that makes me laugh, especially when I note Schiller's smug expression and Izzy rolling her eyes.

"Mama, why is Daddy upset?" Esmeralda, Marco and Izzy's five-year-old daughter says.

"Because he missed his favorite television show last night," Izzy says without missing a beat.

Esmeralda climbs into her father's lap and says solemnly, "There's no shows out in the middle of the ocean, Daddy. You should know that."

Marco tosses his wife a look of exasperation, and says, dropping a kiss to his daughter's head, "You're right, Alda. Daddy should know better."

Connor comes barreling over from his deck cushion. Before any of us can stop him, he yanks a strand of Esmeralda's hair, making her yelp, and cries, "But we *do* have shows on the boat, Alda. We watched one yesterday, remember?"

"Connor!" I bark, "Don't pull her hair. You know better than that. Apologize to her this instant."

But before he has a chance to do so, Esmeralda hauls off and kicks Connor right in the stomach from her perch on her father's lap. Connor doubles over and starts moaning.

"Alda!" Izzy yells, horrified.

Schiller claps a hand over his mouth to stifle a bout of laughter.

"No daughter of mine is going to let boys boss her around, huh?" says Marco, shoulders shaking as he runs a hand through his daughter's hair.

"And no husband of mine is going to *watch television shows* if he keeps encouraging said daughter that violence is okay," Izzy says sweetly, which sobers Marco up real fast.

"Looks like you and I are the only civilized ones here, Iz," I say, striding up to Connor and squeezing his shoulder. "You okay, bud?"

"Yeah," he groans, straightening but still rubbing his stomach.

"Good. Now apologize to her."

Connor stares at me in horror. "She *kicked* me!"

I stare down at my six-year-old. "And you pulled her hair. You both need to apologize."

Connor's face twists in a mutinous little line, then he says, "Sorry, Alda."

Esmeralda sniffles and rubs her face. "Alda!" Izzy says sharply.

"Sorry for kicking you, Connor," she mumbles.

Marco sets her down on the deck. "All right, now the two of you go play together and *stop fighting.*"

Connor takes Esmeralda's hand and tows her back to the cushions. Esmeralda, who's a year younger than Connor, struggles to keep up and yanks on his hand to make him slow down, which he does for about three steps before picking up the pace again.

"God help us when they get older," says Schiller.

Marco sighs. "Please, for the love of God, don't make me think about that until it's absolutely necessary. I'd like to live in denial for as long as possible."

I sink into a chair, then say to my husband, "Where's our other child?"

Schiller shrugs, but Izzy says, "Kit is reading a dive book with Sienna and little Marco in our cabin."

"More like Kit is lecturing the two of them on proper dive procedures now that he can finally read on his own," groans Schiller.

"Comes with being the oldest, I suppose," I say.

Izzy makes a face. "Well, Sienna's eight, too, and could give him a run for his money in bossiness."

"That girl is going to run our company one day," Marco says proudly, "Of course she's bossy."

"Yes, well, for now the only person she can manage to do that to is the four-year-old—and you."

Marco grins widely. "Takes after her father."

Izzy rolls her eyes. "Now there's a statement that's never been truer."

Schiller casts a glance toward the cabin. "I'm surprised Galvan's not awake yet."

I reach over and squeeze his hand. "You know he sleeps a lot now, Schiller, especially in the morning."

Schiller frowns. "Yeah, I do. It's just hard to see him lose his vitality."

"He's getting up there," I say gently. "And the trial took a lot out of him."

Between the two of them, Lachlan and Alastair's trials took the better part of three years to litigate, after all the appeals and delays were over. By then, we'd already had Kit and were working on Connor. Supporting him with our young family was never easy, but we prioritized it, and now that the criminals are officially away for good, he's a permanent fixture on the dive boat Schiller and I bought after we got married.

Schiller still doesn't like to use his inheritance, but with two small kids, he's begun to admit the benefit of having it, especially since it means he can give his children the things his parents never did, which is largely just unconditional love and plenty of dive videos.

We both decided for the sake of our children we would try to fix the relationships with our parents. These days, we're all polite to each other, and the grandparents spoil the boys rotten, but we'll probably never be the super tight-knit family like we see in the movies we watch on movie night.

Schiller must guess the direction of my thoughts

because he smiles a little sadly and throws an arm around my shoulder.

Izzy picks up on our melancholy and changes the subject. "I have to say I'll never get used to this gigantic boat of yours. Thank you again for inviting us despite our poorly-behaved children."

"Yes, well, we appreciate the yearly vacation to the villa in Tuscany," Schiller says dryly, then shakes his head as if he can't believe he's become one of those wealthy people that just go around living in each other's insanely huge estates all the time.

"Happy to oblige," says Marco, raising his mimosa and then taking a hearty sip.

"Morning, folks!"

We turn as Galvan slowly walks out onto the deck. Schiller jumps up and makes to escort him over to the table, but Galvan swats his hand away. "I'm old, Schiller, not an invalid."

Schiller looks like he'd rather pick the man up and deposit him at the table himself, but he says nothing. I pass Galvan a mimosa once he's settled and ask him how he's feeling this morning.

"Oh, fine. Can't complain. In fact, I've been up for a little while. You'll never guess who I just got off the phone with."

"Who?" Schiller asks with interest.

"Made."

"*Really?*" says Schiller, then folds his arms over his chest and stares up at the brilliant sky, the wristband

Galvan bought for him all those years ago glinting in the sunshine. "Hell, I don't think I've called him in nearly a year. How is he?"

"Doing incredibly well. He's been running the Jakarta Interpol field office for five months now."

Schiller blinks in surprise. "Damn, that's great. I still can't believe you demanded he accompany me on that boat as an undercover agent and bodyguard for me."

Galvan shrugs. "By that point, Interpol had egg on their faces for not having put them away after all those years, so they couldn't really deny me the favor, could they? Besides, they were hoping to conduct that deal onboard with the undercover Interpol agents to give them enough evidence to make arrests. Someone had to be placed with the crew before that happened."

Izzy shivers. "Thank God we've never been involved in such a dangerous situation. I don't know how you waited to hear word that Schiller was safe, Pippa. The wait would have killed me if something had happened to Marco."

"It wasn't fun," I say. "But I knew Schiller had Made and Bentley with him, so that helped. How is Bentley, by the way?"

Schiller shrugs. "He's fine. Busy with the company and the wife. And the child, for that matter. You know how much he struggled after his family's company took such a hit from being involved with Alastair's outfit. Their reputation never really recovered."

"Thank God he has Alyssa," I say.

Schiller nods. "She really turned out to be a godsend, didn't she?"

"But that's all over now," Galvan interjects. "Everything worked out in the end."

Schiller grins. "It did—apart from one thing."

Galvan frowns. "What?"

Schiller leans toward us and winks. "We never did find your wreck!"

We all laugh, Galvan the loudest. Once we've finally quieted down, Galvan says, "You know, if you really wanted to know, I could tell you its location. There might still be a piece or two yet to discover at the bottom of the sea."

Schiller glances over to where Kit, Sienna, and little Marco are coming out of the cabin to join Alda and Connor. He smiles again, and this time there's no hint of sadness in his ocean-blue eyes, only happiness. "That might be an adventure for our children one day."

I grin, too. It might just be.

AUTHOR'S NOTE

I had the opportunity to travel to Bali in 2018. It is an incredible place, and the memories I have of it will always be dear to me. Many of the scenes in this story are lifted from my travels, but as an outsider, I cannot know what it is like to live in Bali, and this book is not meant to be taken as such. What follows are a few notes you may find interesting about the story.

First, I hope I've done justice to what it's like to scuba dive. It's a difficult sport, but anyone who is interested can become a certified diver (you can't dive by yourself without being certified.) If diving is something that sounds interesting to you and you want to know how to get started, consider doing a Discovery Dive with PADI, the world's largest certifier of divers and advocate for diving. I got certified through PADI myself.

During a discovery dive, they will attach you to an instructor and take you down without having to go through certification first. This is a great way to determine whether diving is something you will enjoy before making the commitment to get certified. Discovery dives are available at dive outfits all around the world. Note that the courses will differ slightly inside vs. outside the United States much like how the US uses the imperial system vs. the metric system for the rest of the world (e.g. miles vs. kilometers) so if you're going to do most of your diving in the US, you might consider getting certified inside the US.

All that said, it is absolutely critical that any diving you do is through an absolutely safe outfit. I have included a link to PADI's website at the end of this note. You can put in your location or where you'd like to dive/get certified and they will have a list of safe and respected outfits in that location. Do a bunch of research and read all reviews.

Many places in the US will do a certification course over a two-week period of time. I actually don't recommend this, as all the skills can become rusty between classes. I took a 4-and-a-half full day course in the Philippines to become certified, and I believe this was more beneficial to getting the skills solidified in my mind. You can easily find week-long courses throughout the US if you're looking for an interesting trip for you or your family.

After you are certified, it is VERY important to realize that while you are certified down to certain depths, you are still very much a novice diver. Consider finding a local dive group to go on your first dives after becoming certified. Also consider always hiring a dive instructor or dive master to dive with you as you gain experience. Create a plan and *stick to it*. Never deviate. That's how accidents happen. There's a reason Schiller insists on this.

Most importantly, if you're about to dive and you ever feel nervous or uneasy, *don't dive that day*. No matter what anyone else says on the boat. And if people you frequently dive with advise you not to go on a particular dive, don't do it. Other people can have a more objective idea of our abilities. Have fun!

Made is named after the guide we had for part of our trip. He is the person who told me about how people are named in Bali. If you are ever on the island, you can contact him at Made Sugiana Bali Transport.

Sanur is the town where you can catch a boat to Nusa Penida for sightseeing. You can also head to Lombok for great diving. I was not yet certified when I visited Bali, so I can't speak to the diving, but I know it's beautiful.

You may recognize the Moorish Idol fish as "Gill" from *Finding Nemo*. They are proud and independent fish that mate for life, which makes them very difficult to raise in captivity, and even harder to breed. One wonders if the real reason Gill wanted to escape was to get back to his mate.

The Mola mola, also called the ocean sunfish, is truly a weird creature. I have not yet seen one, but they are fairly common around Bali and you MUST watch this video included at the end of this note that has both the Mola mola and Moorish Idol to see how weird it is!

The Tegenungan Waterfall is probably the most famous waterfall in Bali. You've likely seen photos of it all over Instagram. Unfortunately, while the falls are huge, I don't think you can hide behind them, and that goes double for sexy times!

The Rock Bar is a real place at the Ayana Resort in the southern area of the island. I did not have the opportunity to stay at the resort, but we went for dinner and it was incredible. Be sure to get there around four o'clock to see the sunset. It's hard to get a table, so get there early!

- PADI Dive Certification:
  padi.com/education/elearning-programs
- Video of the Mola mola and Moorish idol:
  youtu.be/x-CAXj2KQ4w
- Rock Bar at the Ayana Resort:
  ayana.com/bali/ayana-resort-and-spa/eat-and-drink/venues/rockbar

ALSO BY K.D. ELIZABETH

Construct My Heart Series

Miss InstaPrincess

Miss ManKiller

The Bright Series

The Christmas Cadeau

The Season Bright

Christmas of White

The King Brothers

Monster

Devil

Rascal

The King Cousins

Lush

Rogue

Follow K.D. Elizabeth on Instagram at @kdewrites or visit her website at www.kdewrites.com.

ACKNOWLEDGMENTS

Thanks a bunch to Chad for reading over the dive sections to make sure I got everything right! This was a fun exercise in "how not to dive."

As always, thank you so much, Cassie, for your great work editing! And of course, thanks to Alison of Red Leaf Proofing, for making sure my final text is clean!

A huge shoutout to my lovely street team and everyone who helped promote this book, especially Grey's Promotions. I'm really grateful for the help with the release.

THANK YOU to all my wonderful readers. This book was a fun diversion from my other series and I hope you enjoyed the adventure with me!

Finally, to my family, I so appreciate the love and support you continue to give me.

With love,
K.D. Elizabeth

Made in the USA
Middletown, DE
11 July 2023

34876347R00135